"That wasn't fair, you know."

Mike's voice came out of the darkness from where he'd isolated himself on the extreme far edge of the bed.

"What wasn't fair?" As if she couldn't guess.

"Prancing into my bedroom, half...not even half-dressed, and shivering so hard, your teeth chattered." He shifted closer to the bed's edge. "Just don't forget our deal. As soon as you get warmed up, you get your clothes on and leave. In the meantime, you stay over there, and I stay over here."

"Do you really hate having me here that much?"

Their breathing filled the silence.

"Mike?"

"I'm thinking."

What the hell was he thinking about? Despair danced around her like the firelight shadows flitting over the ceiling. Jackie Barrett, hapless harlot, sorry siren. If she didn't do something quick, she'd be right back out in the snow....

Dear Reader,

Once upon a time we were little girls dreaming of handsome princes on white chargers, of fairy godmothers who'd made us into beautiful princesses and of mountain castles where we'd live happily ever after.

Now that we're all grown up, we can recapture those dreams in a brand-new miniseries, ONCE UPON A KISS. It features stories based on some of the world's best-loved fairy tales—expressly for the little girl who still lives on inside of us.

This month, Elizabeth Sinclair brings you *Eight Men and a Lady*, a contemporary retelling of *Snow White and the Seven Dwarfs*. Elizabeth loves to hear from her readers. Write to her at: P.O. Box 840084, St. Augustine, FL 32084-0084. Or E-mail her at: M.Smith 132@genie.com

Be sure to read all six of our wonderful fairy-tale romances, coming to you every other month, only from American Romance!

ONCE UPON A KISS—at the heart of every little girl's dreams...and every woman's fantasies...

Happy Reading!

Debra Matteucci
Senior Editor & Editorial Coordinator
Harlequin
300 East 42nd Street
New York, New York 10017

Elizabeth Sinclair

EIGHT MEN AND A LADY

Harlequin Books

TORONTO • NEW YORK • LONDON
AMSTERDAM • PARIS • SYDNEY • HAMBURG
STOCKHOLM • ATHENS • TOKYO • MILAN
MADRID • WARSAW • BUDAPEST • AUCKLAND

To the Halos, for the use of their names
and that river of love.
To Edna, for her faith in me. I love you, Mom.
And as always, to my husband, Bob, with love.

ISBN 0-373-16677-X

EIGHT MEN AND A LADY

Copyright © 1997 by Marguerite Smith.

Chapter One

The pungent odor of raw fish dragged Jacqueline Barrett from her deep slumber. Her eyelids fluttered open.

Slowly, the fog of sleep cleared to reveal a circle of bearded men gathered around her bed. She gasped, hauled the multicolored quilt up to her chin, then scooted backward, plastering herself against the headboard of the single bed.

Wide-eyed, she stared back into a sea of gray hair and hovering faces, praying this was a nightmare from which she'd awaken to find herself still in her brother's rented Adirondack fishing cabin.

She blinked experimentally.

The faces remained in place, nearly blocking out the rough-hewn log walls, the uncurtained windows and the fieldstone fireplace with its cross-eyed, moth-eaten moose head glaring down at her.

Unquestionably, a man's domain.

Unfortunately, and to Jackie's peril, in her haste to erase the blinding exhaustion of her long drive, she hadn't locked the front door or even noticed if it had a lock.

She shuddered. Who'd have thought she'd meet her end at the liver-spotted hands of a gang of Medicare marauders?

As they closed their ranks and intensified their overt inspection of her, indignation at being once more the center of unwanted attention overrode her fear. If death had chosen this moment to claim her, serenely wouldn't be the way she'd go.

In the past two months, she'd hidden in ladies' rooms from the persistent media, smiled sweetly at and turned down marriage proposals from leering fortune hunters. She'd fended off a battalion of new-found "friends," outwitted clever scam artists and in general watched her quiet, well-ordered life turn topsy-turvy. Now, she'd found a haven. Was she supposed to just give it up without a fight?

No.

She'd never backed down from a fight in her life. And now, when her sanity depended on it, was not the time to start. She loosened her stranglehold on the quilt and opened her mouth to register an outraged protest.

"Humph! A woman!" The rude grunt emanated from the vicinity of her feet.

"Yeah. She's a woman, all right." A swooning sigh followed the breathy statement of the teenager who'd elbowed his way between two of the older men.

Jackie followed his adolescent leer to the twin mounds pushing against the front of her green cashmere sweater. Obviously suffering from acne as well as a bad case of stampeding hormones, he appeared to see her as a hot fudge sundae and himself as a chocoholic.

With the exception of the one man glaring at her from the foot of the bed, they all chuckled. Their amusement fired her indignation into full flame.

Enough already!

She'd spent weeks providing entertainment for every inquisitive Tom, Dick and Harry who came down the pike. She'd had it. Was a little peace and quiet too damn much to ask?

Throwing her mane of blond curls over her shoulder, she stiffened her spine, stuck her chin out a notch and prepared for battle.

"Who are you? What do you want? And why are you in my cabin?"

Her voice rose with each question, adopting the same tone she saved for her brother Dave. Since his latest blunder had messed up her life, she'd perfected the dramatic overtones.

"Humph!"

The disgruntled expletive came from the same man who only moments before had so expertly identified her gender. He stood ramrod straight at the end of the bed, forehead furrowed, arms crossed over his broad chest like an offended little general. An abundant crop of snowy hair capped his head, and she amended his honorary title to Retired Little General.

"Did you hear that? *Her* cabin? *She* invades our territory and declares a victory before we hit the beachhead."

"Now, now, Peppy. Give the poor child a chance to explain." The gentling words, uttered by the older man standing beside the ogling teenager, calmed her some.

A warm brown-eyed gaze sparkled down at her over the gold-rimmed spectacles teetering on the end of his nose. With a practiced flick of his finger, he set the glasses back in place and smiled. "I'm afraid there's been a mistake, my dear. You see, this is our cabin. Now, if you'll tell us your name, we'll try to find out where you belong."

"Jacqueline Barrett. Jackie," she blurted out, remembering too late to use the alias she and Dave had dreamed up. "And you're the ones who've made the mistake. My brother rented this cabin for a month and loaned it to me."

A sudden thought struck her. Maybe *Dave* had made the mistake. Not an unheard-of possibility. Lately, he'd made a career of screwing things up big time. "Perhaps he meant one of the other cabins?" The certainty in her voice had begun to wane.

The bespectacled man looked to the others, then back to her and smiled sympathetically. "I'm afraid there aren't any other cabins available. The camp is undergoing renovations. At present, this is the only one rented out. Who did you say made your reservations?"

Her uneasiness at having revealed her name turned to wonder. Didn't these guys have newspapers here? Obviously not, or one of them surely would have recognized her name.

The tension she'd grown so accustomed to over the past two months slipped a bit, taking with it a good portion of her indignation.

Smiling wearily, she examined the faces staring down at her. No matter who shouldered the blame, there had been a mistake, all right. And the warning bells going off in her head had a decidedly familiar ring.

In her mind, this "little oversight" ranked right up there with the others for which Dave had earned his recent notoriety as a world-class blockhead. There could be no other logical explanation for how she'd ended up in a mountain cabin with....

She counted them. *Seven? Seven men?*

Good grief, she'd awakened smack-dab in the middle of a fairy tale.

Her predicament was almost laughable. Almost. The only amusement she could find in her situation at the moment, however, came from the thought of having Dave's mouth sewn shut—permanently.

"I'm really sorry about this. My brother Dave—"

"Dave? Dave Barrett?" the friendly, bespectacled old man asked suddenly. She nodded. "So you're Dave's sister. He talks about you all the time."

Jackie cringed. Dave's penchant for talking too much about her to the wrong people had perpetrated this little fiasco.

"He gave up his reservation so I could use the cabin and get a little...rest." No point in telling them Dave's benevolent gesture had come as a result of overwhelming guilt for making her life hell, compounded by her outrage at finding he'd donated her entire wardrobe to charity and replaced it with designer clothes. Lord, if she didn't love her only brother, she'd....

"Humph!" Peppy grunted. "He always manages to slip a woman in to screw up our fishing trips. Last time, a dancing girl popped out of Doc's birthday cake. Miracle she didn't catch pneumonia, what with nothing covering her but tassels and fringe. Took us three days to get rid of her."

"Speak for yourself. Some of us had other plans for her." The remark, flavored by a heavy New York accent, came from a man at the side of the bed sporting a black beard and a rakish grin. Closer to Dave's thirty-eight years than to his senior companions, he had an olive complexion and dark eyes that hinted at a Latin ancestry.

"Stow it, Tony," the ill-tempered man snapped. "We should have come this year without telling Barrett. Leave it to him to mess things up. Boy's got no brains, bringing that dancer here with only a cork and two Band-Aids in her suitcase." He arched an eyebrow in Jackie's general direction. "And now *her*."

Despite herself, she snickered, but Peppy's glare effectively harnessed her mirth.

"That's my brother. If it's any consolation, ever since I graduated from diapers to training pants he's been managing to mess up my life quite nicely. In fact—" She stopped herself just short of spilling more than she wanted anyone to know about her.

She should have known this wouldn't be as simple

as Dave had made it out to be. With the exception of giving her the job as head chef at his restaurant, his harebrained schemes always had a price. Unfortunately, she always got stuck with the tab. For a moment, she amused herself with the idea of hiring a hit man to remove the only son of Mildred and Charles Barrett from her life.

"My, my. We seem to have a problem here," the soft-spoken Doc mused aloud.

We sure do, and its name is Dave Barrett.

"It would seem the young lady belongs here, after all." Doc flicked his glasses back in place and turned to the others. "I don't see that we can do anything about it."

"Can, too," Peppy cut in. "We can throw her out bag and baggage. Let her make camp somewhere else. There's enough hotels around here."

Panic rose in Jackie like a spring flood. She couldn't leave. These guys had no idea who she was. She'd found anonymity again. What were her chances of finding another place where no one knew her? What were the chances that some other place wouldn't plunge her back into the public eye? Nil, that's what they were.

Her luck had run out when that busty, grinning blonde had pulled those six numbered plastic balls from those bins.

No! She *would not* go back to being a curiosity.

"Please. I won't be a bother. You won't even know I'm here." She glanced wildly around the room, noticing for the first time the piles of haphazardly discarded clothes, the dusty kitchenette and the rows of unmade beds. "I'll take care of the place. You know, pick up, straighten things, dust...."

Had she just volunteered to keep house for seven men? At what point had she lost her mind? Oh, hells bells, if they let her stay, what difference did a little work make? She pressed her lips tightly together before she added vacuuming and made a total ass of herself.

Cooking for them had entered her mind, too, just to sweeten the deal. But the thought of their running to the nearest newspaper and proclaiming that Jacqueline Barrett, the only winner of the largest lottery jackpot in New York State history, was holed up in an Adirondack Mountain fishing camp with seven men squelched the idea before it reached her loose lips.

She looked hopefully from one hairy face to the other.

"Don't need you cleaning anything," Peppy snapped. "If we wanted our quarters shipshape, we'd do it ourselves." He turned to Doc. "Put it to a vote, Doc. I say she goes."

"Vote it is." After sending Jackie an apologetic look, Doc turned to the man who had drifted away from the group and stretched out on a nearby cot. "Rip?"

Rip folded his arms behind his head and studied Jackie through slitted eyes. She flashed him her most bewitching smile. His lips quirked slightly in response. "Aw, let her stay. What's the big deal?" Moments later, as if he'd found the effort of making a decision too exhausting, his breathy snores filled the gap in conversation.

Jackie looked at Doc in wonder. "Rip? As in Van Winkle?"

He nodded. "Name's Bill. He's revitalizing his system," Doc explained matter-of-factly.

Revitalizing it for what?

He turned to the next man, apparently used to this turn of events. "Tony?"

The black-bearded Latino chuckled. "You're askin' me if I wanna keep a dame around?" He laughed outright. "Does a bear—"

Doc's admonishing scowl cut him short. "We get the idea, Tony. Adam, what's your vote?"

Adam, a red-nosed, spindly little man, opened his mouth to cast his vote. Before a word passed his lips, his eyes squeezed shut, his nose quivered like a rabbit's, then curled against his top lip.

Someone thrust a handkerchief into his hand. He plastered the white material under his nose. "Ah...Ah...Ahhh."

The long sigh, Jackie surmised, signaled the abatement of the sneeze. Stuffing the handkerchief in his pocket, he mumbled in a nasally voice, "Let her stay," then sneezed, anyway.

"Cold's sounding better, Adam. Don't forget to keep taking that medicine I prescribed. Harold?"

Jackie smiled at the color that rose in Harold's face. He bowed his head, stared fixedly at his feet over a large spare-tire middle, glanced at Jackie, then averted his gaze and nodded.

Skipping over the scowling Peppy, Doc threw his arm around the teenager's slim shoulders. "Tommy? What do you think? Does she stay or does she go?"

Tommy's undivided attention hadn't left Jackie for a second. Reminding her of a puppy drooling over a bone, he nodded eagerly, sending the pompon on his green knit cap into a comical dance. His ears blushed pink. "Yeah, Gramps. Let her stay. She won't be any trouble. I promise. I'll fix a place for her. I can tack a blanket to one of the beams so she can have her own room."

Jackie felt like a stray dog the family had adopted and allotted a bed made from Granny's old house dress in the corner of the garage.

"Well, my dear, it looks as if you're staying," Doc announced with a wide grin.

"Thank you. You won't be sorry."

"Humph!" Peppy glared at each of them in turn, stomped to the door, then flung it open. "You'll be sorry. Mark my words. When Mike finds out about this, he won't be any happier about having a darn female around here than I am—especially a rich one." Using unnecessary vigor for punctuation, Peppy slammed the door shut behind him.

MIKE HAMILTON assessed the large, dead pine tree leaning against the cabin roof, then shook his head. Every time he got one repair done, three more cropped up. His bank account looked like roadkill, and with reservations hitting rock bottom this winter, he didn't see any hope of inflating it, unless the bank came through with that second mortgage. And the bank president had said Mike had a fifty-fifty chance.

In the meantime, he'd have to go on patching and repairing. Today, the first order of business entailed removing that tree before its weight caved in the roof. Well, at least it would cut down on his fuel bill, he thought, looking on the bright side. If he could get Tommy to give him a hand, he'd have it done before lunch.

After lunch, he'd tackle the patch work on one of the cabins. That would leave only four more to repair. Once the bank approved the second mortgage, he'd be able to hire someone to help him with the work. By the time spring rolled around, he'd be home-free and ready for a full roster of guests. The thought of Land's End teeming with spring trout fishermen made him smile.

Peering up at the swaying pines and the clear blue sky, he grinned. Things were definitely showing signs of going his way—finally. Even the weather had cleared. Nothing could spoil his mood today, not even a sixty-foot dead pine tree.

Rounding the corner of the big cabin to search for Tommy, he stopped short of walking into the side of a little red Porsche convertible. For a moment, he admired its sleek lines. A far cry from his tired, old white pickup.

He wondered who it belonged to. All his regular guests knew the rules about parking only in the lot next to the main lodge. Had to be a visitor. He ran a loving, envious hand over the gleaming fender, walked past it, then bounded up the stairs to the cabin's front door.

As he mounted the first step, the door flew open. Had he not done a quick sidestep, Peppy would have run him down.

"Is the draft board after you?"

"Wish it were that simple," Peppy grumbled, stabbing at the air over his shoulder with his thumb. "Just take a gander inside." The retired air force colonel snatched up his tackle box from the pile of discarded fishing gear near the door, then marched off toward the frozen lake.

Mike stared after him. Peppy's deep, authoritative voice continued to warn Mike about *someone,* then something about *their* shenanigans before his words trailed off into silence.

Laughing to himself at Peppy's muttering, Mike took the remaining few stairs two at a time.

Shoving open the door, he stepped inside and waited for his eyes to adjust to the dim interior. The smell of fish and fresh-brewed coffee assaulted his nose. Slowly the group of men huddled in a tight circle at the far side of the room came into focus. He reached behind him and pulled the door shut. The man stretched out on the bed never flinched.

Five heads pivoted toward him.

"Mike!" Doc separated himself from the group. The remaining four immediately closed ranks.

"Hi, fellas. What's up? Peppy says there's something in here I should see. And if it's a repair, I really don't want to hear about it." He smiled to soften the words.

"By the way, did Barrett ever make it to camp?" He hoped so. Otherwise he'd have to dig up some cash for a refund.

"No. No repairs." Doc glanced at the others, then back at Mike. His grin broadened. "I guess you could say Barrett arrived."

Muffled snickers rippled from the direction of the men.

Mike glanced their way, then back to Doc. "Well, I hope that fancy car out there isn't his. He knows the rules about guest parking." Mike stretched to peer over Doc's shoulder at the tight circle of men acting as if they'd been glued together at the hip and shoulder. "What's going on?"

Four moronic smiles flashed in answer.

Doc grabbed the pot from the stove and held it up in invitation. "Uh, coffee, Mike?"

The tantalizing aroma of the fresh-brewed coffee wafted toward Mike, but he shook his head and scanned the room for clues as to what they were up to. His gaze fell on a pile of expensive suitcases stacked near the fireplace. The men normally came with more fishing gear than clothes and none of it typically came packed in anything labeled Gucci. The luggage piqued his curiosity. "Barrett's traveling a little heavy this season, isn't he?"

"Uh, yes and no." Setting the coffeepot back on the stove, Doc cleared his throat, pushed his glasses back on his nose, then slipped his hand in his trouser pocket. "Dave isn't here…exactly."

Mike captured Doc's wandering gaze with a frown. "What do you mean *exactly*? Either he's here or he isn't. Which is it?"

"Well…"

"I'm the Barrett who arrived."

Pivoting sharply toward the wall of men, Mike stared. Though handsome men for the most part, not a one of them had the face and figure to match that voice. Unless he'd lost it completely, that sound had come from a woman. "Who said that?"

"I did."

As if reenacting Moses parting the Red Sea, the men slowly separated. A woman sat cross-legged in the middle of the bed. Mike caught his breath. If a bull moose had charged his midsection, it would have had less of an impact than this woman's beauty.

Her blond hair parted in the center above a high forehead, then cascaded past her shoulders like a waterfall with the sun shining on it. Eyes, blue as the mountain lakes, challenged him from a face he quickly rated as the loveliest he'd ever seen and holding all the promise of a yellow dog-toothed violet pushing through the snow. She made the whole place seem even shabbier.

Mike squared his shoulders, pulled his jacket closed to ward off the strange, tingly chill racing over him, then crossed his arms over his chest.

"I'm Dave's sister, Jacqueline. He let me take his

place this year. If it's going to be a problem, I can pay extra."

The unspoken defiance in her eyes took Mike by surprise. Did she expect him to throw her out? He stepped closer, allowing his gaze to drift down to her cashmere sweater and her raw silk slacks.

Damn! He didn't know Dave had a sister, much less a rich one. His good mood soured. His body cooled, as if doused with ice water.

Everything in him rebelled instantly against her presence, her fancy car, her expensive clothes, her money. No. Not her money. He didn't give a rat's patootie about her money.

What abraded his good mood was the haughty attitude that always came with wealth. That I-can-do-anything-I-want-and-get-away-with-it-because-I'm-rich persona mirrored in that streak of defiance shining in her eyes. Well, not around here she couldn't, and definitely not around him.

"No need. We charge the same for everybody." He gestured toward the stack of suitcases. "I suppose that luggage and the Porsche outside belong to you." He didn't even try to hide the disdain in his voice.

He'd spent enough summers busing tables at some of the nearby resorts to know fancy designer clothes when he saw them. He'd also seen how these city girls dazzled the mountain boys with their wealth, played with their hearts, then hurried back to their charity luncheons and cocktail parties, never caring or seeing the men they left destroyed and broken.

His brother Ken had learned that the hard way. If

it hadn't been for that.... No. Mike wouldn't allow her to resurrect that pain. He'd buried that a long time ago, with Ken.

"Guilty."

Her voice roused him from unwanted thoughts. A slow smile worked its way across her full, lush mouth.

He stared at her. Arrows of awareness shot to all his nerve endings. That vulnerability stung. He deliberately shut it down before it reached his eyes.

"A word of warning, *Jacqueline*. You're in for a very dull four weeks. This fishing camp doesn't provide entertainment for its guests." His voice emerged much colder than he'd intended, but when she started at his words, he pressed his advantage. "All we do here is fish."

Her smile vanished. Cold reserve took its place. Chin elevated, she lowered her legs over the side of the cot and stood. "I didn't come here expecting to be entertained, Mr.... "

Her gaze bored into him. Reading. Measuring. Probing. Feeling invaded, he quickly filled in the blank for her, effectively averting her attention.

"Hamilton. Mike Hamilton. I own the camp."

She threw an evaluating glance around the dingy room. "Yes. Well, *Mr. Mike Hamilton*, you can go to bed with a clear conscience tonight. I've been providing my own entertainment for some time now."

The men stayed clear of the conversation, following the exchange as if watching a tennis match. Every one of them still wore the same cow-eyed expression they'd had when he walked through the door.

Obviously, she had them snowed already. He turned his attention back to the woman.

Been providing her own entertainment, huh?

"I'm sure you have."

As his words hit their mark, the look of haughty superiority slipped from her expression, replaced by— Was that hurt? He excused his rude behavior by reminding himself that most of the rich female tourists knew their way around, be it Lord and Taylor or a stranger's bedroom. The reminder did little to salve his biting conscience.

In spite of that, a deeper, more personal hurt pushed him to add one parting shot. "And while you're at it, park that car where it belongs. You'll have to get used to walking from the guest parking lot, just like everyone else. Our parking attendant has the day off."

When she bristled, he knew he'd struck pay dirt and waited for the reward of satisfaction. Oddly enough, he felt only self-reproach. Exactly when had he become such a bastard? And when had he started treating guests as if they were expendable?

The answers came swift and true. When he'd found this rich socialite had invaded his camp and dredged up memories he never wanted to face again.

He had to get the hell out of here before he said or did something he'd really be sorry for.

"The car will be moved directly." She fished a ring of keys from an expensive, brown leather handbag.

Tommy stumbled forward, grinning ear to ear. "I'll move it for you, Jackie."

"Thank you." Smiling sweetly at the young boy, she dropped the keys into his outstretched palm, then glared at Mike. "Are there any other rules I'm breaking?"

For a long, tension-packed moment, Mike held her sky-blue gaze with his. *Yes, you're too beautiful, too tempting, too sexy, too...*

She blinked, breaking the spell. The hurt and confusion reflected in her eyes contradicted her sarcasm and cut deep, right down to the soles of his feet. Guilt pummeled him. He'd had no real cause to be so rough on her. He opened his mouth to apologize.

She tilted her head and the diamond stud in her left ear flashed a warning at him.

Save your apologies for someone who deserves them, Hamilton. Diamond earrings, leather luggage, cashmere sweaters, a Porsche? This woman hardly needs apologies or pity. Just because she's beautiful is no reason to lose your head. She's cut from the same cloth as the other rich tourists who come to the mountains to play. Besides, even if she isn't like the rest, it would take a rocket ship to reach her—if you wanted to—which you don't.

"See you later, fellas. I've got a missing waitress and cook to round up and a tree waiting to be cut down." Suddenly eager to escape the elusive drift of expensive perfume, which registered foreign to these male quarters and annoyed him beyond logical reason, he moved quickly to the door. Poised with his hand on the knob, he turned to Doc.

"By the way, tell Peppy I called his wife. I knew

he'd forget and she'd worry until she knew he'd arrived okay.'' Unable to resist one more glimpse at Jackie, he exited the cabin.

The door slammed shut. Jackie stared at it with a mutinous glare. Her knees sagged. She dropped to the edge of the bed. Their confrontation had taken the starch from her.

''You have a nice day, too, jerk,'' she mumbled.

Who did that opinionated, overbearing, pompous Paul Bunyon think he was? Looking like a cross between Tom Cruise and Adonis didn't give him the right to treat her like an ant at a candymakers' picnic. Just because he had more muscle than the seams of his sheepskin jacket could hold didn't mean she would grovel at his feet for permission to stay in his fishing camp. And if he thought for one minute that he could suck her in with his blazing semisweet chocolate eyes, his carved cheekbones and his silky black hair, he had another think coming. So he'd been thoughtful enough to make sure Peppy's wife didn't worry about him—so what?

The man had no social skills and the disposition of a constipated toad. She didn't need that kind of complication in her life right now, even if she had read interest in his eyes. Though *interest* hardly characterized the blatantly sexual undertones flashing from those inky depths. Even with him glaring at her, her body had reacted to him with astounding strength. She didn't even try to kid herself into believing he wasn't attractive— or that she wasn't attracted.

Having spent the better part of the past few years

learning to be a top-notch chef, she knew delicious when she saw it, and this guy went far beyond that. She also knew that no matter how tempting a dish appeared, the calories could also be lethal, clogging arteries with rich fat and bringing on heart attacks. Heart problems she didn't need, especially the kind generated by an ill-tempered fishing camp entrepreneur with a chip on his shoulder the size of a giant Sequoia and a gleam in his eye that would make Don Juan blush.

A gentle hand came to rest on her shoulder. "Don't let Mike get to you. His bark's a lot worse than his bite. He's really a nice guy and quite harmless."

Jackie gazed up into Doc's kindly face. "So are tigers, when they're kept behind bars." The bed gave under his weight as he settled his bulk beside her. She frowned. "Is Mike upset because I came in my brother's place?"

"Of course not." Doc patted her hand still balled in a rebellious fist in her lap. "Right now, Mike can use the money. From you or from Dave, makes no difference." Doc glanced toward the door through which Mike had disappeared. "What that boy really needs is a lot less tangible than money…and a lot harder to come by."

"What he *really* needs?"

Doc sprang to his feet with amazing agility for a man his size. "How would you like to do some ice fishing?"

The corners of Jackie's mouth curved in appreciation. *Nice sidestep, Doc.* Okay. She wouldn't push for answers. After all, it was none of her business what Mike Hamilton needed. Then again, from that look in his eyes when he'd checked her out, she could make an educated guess—and Jackie Barrett had no intention of providing it.

Right now, she had to worry about what *she* needed, and finding a deserving home for that money she'd won so she could find a little peace of mind. Getting her life back on track came next in line. That's what she had to concentrate on, and what better time to start than now?

"I've never been fishing, with or without ice."

"Get changed and we'll show you how it's done, right, Adam?" Doc waited for the slender, red-beaked man to finish blowing his nose. Adam nodded eagerly.

Jackie glanced down at her designer clothes. Thanks to Dave's guilty conscience, her wardrobe now consisted of garments fashioned with a weekend in the Hamptons in mind, not a fishing camp. And certainly not in the middle of a frozen lake with an Arctic wind whistling around her. She'd only taken the clothes and the car because he'd looked so repentant about accidentally revealing her identity to a restaurant patron who happened to be a reporter for the *New York Times*. The next day, her picture had taken up more room on the front page than the White House dinner for Princess Di.

A long sigh issued from her. Staying angry at Dave would solve nothing. The damage he'd done couldn't be undone. And it *had* been an accident.

Angry or not, she couldn't help thinking about her comfortable jeans and sloppy sweats that Dave had swept from her closet without her permission. Clothes that now resided in a Woodstock thrift shop. *Thank you very much, Dave.*

In his haste to hustle her off to the mountains and ease his conscience, he'd not only bought the clothes, he'd also packed them, then crammed them and her into the car before she could even protest. Wonder if *Field and Stream* offered any prizes for Best-Dressed Fisherman of the Year?

"I'm afraid I didn't come equipped to go fishing. As far as clothes go, this is about it." She swept a hand down her torso.

Adam stepped forward. "I brought some extra gear. You're welcome to use it, if you'd like." He sneezed into his handkerchief, then smiled at her apologetically. "I get a cold every year when I come here. I think the germs lie in wait for me to arrive."

Jackie smiled commiseratively, preparing to gracefully refuse his offer. Then she considered the alternative of sitting in the cabin and stewing over Mike's treatment as well as her own troubles. Just the thought depressed her. "Okay. You're on. But I'd better warn you, I've never even held a fishing pole, much less dangled a worm under a fish's nose."

Adam grinned, his expression transforming from studious to pure delight. "First lesson. Fish don't have noses. Second. We use tip-ups. Although you can use jig poles to fish through the ice."

"Tip-ups? Jig poles?"

Doc showed his sensitivity by not laughing. Instead he crossed his index fingers and explained. "A tip-up's an arrangement of three sticks. Two cross over the hole to keep the tip-up from falling in. The third sticks up and has a spring-loaded flag. The rod the flag is on is triggered by a wire attached to the reel. When a fish takes the bait, the trigger releases and the flag pops up." He looked at her expectantly. "Tip...up?"

Faced with what she knew had to be her expression of total confusion, he patted her shoulder. "Never mind. You'll see soon enough. Adam and I'll teach you everything you need to know."

"But don't I need a license or something?"

The door crashed open, letting in a gust of frigid air. All gazes turned toward the noise. Tommy, seeing his grandfather's admonishing scowl, quickly closed the door, then, before handing her the keys, flashed Jackie a goofy smile.

He hurried off to rummage through a toolbox standing open on the floor. Brandishing a hammer in their direction, he grabbed a blanket off a nearby bed, then headed for the only corner in the room that boasted a window. A few minutes later, the room resonated with the sound of his tacking the blanket to an overhead beam.

"You can get a fishing license from Mike later," Doc yelled above the din.

Dismissing his grandson with a shake of his head, he slipped on a brown weatherproof jacket with a zillion pockets. Pinned to the lapel of one was a gro-

tesque red plastic worm with hooks hanging from its
rump, if that's what you called that end of a worm.

She really wished he hadn't mentioned Mike.
While Jackie found great satisfaction in the complete
acceptance by the majority of the men who would be
her cabin buddies for the next month, Mike's less than
hospitable reaction to her presence still irritated her
beyond reason.

She looked from Doc to Adam and gritted her
teeth. Mike Hamilton could take his grizzly-bear disposition and put it where the sun don't shine. He
wasn't going to ruin the first peace and quiet she'd
known in weeks.

She accepted the clothes offered by Adam, and
while she slipped them on in the cozy alcove Tommy's noise had produced, she plotted her revenge.
She'd catch the biggest fish in the darn lake, then
she'd drop it, slime and all, into Mike Hamilton's
pompous lap.

Parking attendant, indeed!

She'd been parking her own car since she'd learned
to drive. Who needed Mike Hamilton? Who cared
that his fishing camp teetered on the edge of being
condemned? What difference did it make to her that
he had the social skills of a rattlesnake wrapped up
in the sleek pelt of a mountain lion?

The insinuating clang of metal against wood broke
through her rebellious thoughts. Pulling the curtain
aside, she glanced out the window to see Mike atop
an aluminum extension ladder leaning against the roof
of the neighboring cabin.

He'd discarded the heavy sheepskin jacket and replaced it with a down vest, then rolled his blue-and-green-plaid flannel shirt sleeves to his elbows, exposing his thick forearms. Mesmerized, she studied his surefooted ascent up the ladder to the roof's peak. The muscles in his arms and thighs bunched and released like a beating heart.

Mike appeared to be carefully distributing his weight on both feet. Bracing himself, he grabbed the pull cord on the chain saw he'd hauled up with him. Suddenly, he paused, tilting his head to look at something in the fallen tree.

He balanced the saw on the corner of the chimney, then reached into the evergreen boughs with both hands. Not until he'd turned toward her could she see that he cradled a bird's nest. The delicate tangle of leaves, twigs and string looked incongruous in his large hands.

She waited for him to crush it and toss it aside. But he didn't. Instead, he gently laid it on the corner of the brickwork, next to the chain saw.

Maneuvering himself closer to the chimney, he reached for the saw.

His foot slipped.

Jackie's breath stopped.

He slid back down the roof, catching himself before plummeting over the edge. Jackie let out a long relieved sigh. Shinnying his way back up to the peak, he straddled the roof's crest, jeans stretching invitingly over his buns, clinging like lichen on a tree trunk, outlining, molding, tempting. Made a girl want to...

Jackie tore her gaze away, plucked up her sweater and slacks from the floor, then threw them with all her strength on the bed.

The damn man's turning me into a voyeur!

Chapter Two

"Here we go again!"

Mike stared down at the fresh sets of footprints leading up to the building. He set the chain saw atop the snowbank piled against the building's wall, then stepped cautiously over the threshold of the boathouse. The darkened, musty interior reminded him of a tomb.

On silent feet, he eased his way toward the boat resting in the wooden storage cradle. The craft, a small runabout with a compact cutty cabin up front, was to have been his brother Ken's man-toy. Even though Ken had never finished rebuilding it, Mike couldn't have disposed of it any more than he could have closed the doors to Land's End after Ken's death. Someday, when he had time, he'd finish it.

Someone had to remember Ken. The rich bitch driving the car in which Ken died hadn't. She'd gotten her high-powered lawyers to take care of the D.W.I. charges, then skipped out without so much as a sympathy card to excuse the fact that she'd killed a human being with her irresponsible behavior.

Years of treading these floors automatically guided Mike around any telltale squeaks that would give away his presence. Easing up beside the elevated boat, he balled his hand into a fist and punched the side of the half-painted hull.

"Sam, Annie, you in there?"

The boat shuddered. A series of muffled gasps emanated from the interior of the cabin. Sounds of scrambling feet and shuffling bodies followed. Taking a step back, he folded his arms over his chest and waited, listening to the frantic whispers from within the boat's hull. A head of tousled brown hair rose cautiously above the gunnel.

"Mike! Er...Mr. Hamilton!" Land's End's cook, Sam Crenshaw, a wide-eyed young man in his early twenties, peered down at Mike. Sam raked his hand through his hair, trying in vain, while avoiding the leveling glare Mike directed at him, to bring order to the unruly brown thatch.

Mike geared up for his usual lecture to the couple, the same one he delivered each time they had to be rounded up to do their jobs. Before he began, he waited for the inevitable appearance of Sam's companion, Annie, the waitress Mike had hired a couple of months ago. They'd been inseparable for the past several weeks and, as always in the case of first love, oblivious to the world around them.

"You said no one would find us here, Sam." The distinctly feminine voice preceded the emergence of a heart-shaped face framed in undisciplined inky curls. "Mr. Hamilton."

"Hello, Annie."

She shied away, then hid herself behind Sam, peering over his shoulder at Mike, as if he embodied all the hounds of Hades.

Mike sighed. Her timidity always reminded him of Shag, the baby deer he and Ken had rescued from a bear trap and spent an entire summer nursing back to health just after Ken bought the camp. Ken had loved the deer, but Mike trained it to eat from his hand long after Ken's initial interest had waned.

Sam grinned sheepishly, then shrugged.

Rearranging his expression to look as stern as he dared, and with Annie's eyes growing bigger by the minute, Mike tapped his fingertip against the face of his gold watch. "I'll be expecting both of you in the kitchen in five minutes with something cooking other than your hormones."

The young cook extracted himself from the girl's embrace, bounced to his feet, his face flaming, then catapulted over the gunnel of the boat.

"Yes, sir. I'll have supper started in no time, sir." He glanced at his girlfriend, then back to Mike. "I'm sorry about this, Mr. Hamilton. We only came down here to find a little privacy and to have somewhere quiet to talk." He shuffled his feet. "I guess the time kinda got away from us."

Privacy, huh?

Sam made it sound as if they lived in the middle of Times Square. This was the Adirondacks. Trees. Rocks. Mountains. Lakes. Miles of wilderness. Privacy lurked around every corner and bush.

Suppressing another grin, Mike nodded, then pointed to a purplish quarter-size blotch on Sam's neck. "You might want to do something to cover that."

Sam's hand flew to the telling hickey just above his collar. "Uh, sure. I think I have some small bandages in my room."

"Not *too* small, I hope."

Mike suppressed another smile and stepped back to allow Sam room to help Annie down from her precarious perch on the cradle brace. He reminded Mike of a young Ken in so many ways—comb-defying hair, too much body to handle, testosterone locked in stampede mode.

Sam reached up to the pretty young woman with both hands outstretched. She in turn looked down at him with adoring eyes and slipped forward trustingly into his grasp. He eased his burden to the floor with all the care he'd give fine china. Her light perfume, redolent of youth and promise, drove the boathouse's mustiness from Mike's nostrils.

A wave of longing engulfed him. An unexpected craving that called out for someone special, someone who could share his life, took him totally off guard. He averted his gaze from the young couple, suddenly pained by their obvious happiness.

Now what had brought on that foolishness? With the bankruptcy of Land's End breathing down his neck, he needed to stay focused. Keeping the camp afloat took his full concentration. He had no time for relationships.

Nor did he have time to run around searching for his waitress and cook on a daily basis. Hell, if he knew the difference between a colander and coriander, he'd do the cooking himself and save some money.

He should have been reading Sam and Annie the riot act, but he didn't have the heart. What real harm had they done? They were in love. They had their future to look forward to. Why embarrass either of them any further?

"Are we still going to the movies tonight?" The softly spoken words of the young woman clinging to Sam's side broke into Mike's thoughts.

"Gosh, Annie, I don't think so. I'm tapped out." Throwing an embarrassed glance over his shoulder at Mike, Sam guided her gently toward the door. "Can we talk about this later?"

Painfully aware of the less-than-adequate paycheck he gave Sam each week, Mike strode toward them.

"Sam?" Mike dug into his pocket and withdrew a bill. Handing it to Sam, he smiled at them. "Have a good time on me—*after* supper's on the table," he added, punctuating the air in front of their faces with a warning finger.

Sam's eyes grew wide, then his full mouth broke into a grin. "Gee, thanks, Mr. Hamilton." He tucked the bill in his jacket pocket.

"Mike. And don't be too quick to thank me. It'll come out of your paycheck," he added, biting down on the lie.

"Thanks, Mike." Sam turned back to his girlfriend. "Let's go. We got work to do." He grabbed her hand, tugging her toward the main lodge. "This is the last time you'll have to look for us," he called over his shoulder.

Until tomorrow, Mike thought, coming to terms with the inevitable.

Annie slipped her hand free and hung back. She smiled anxiously at Mike, then raised on tiptoe and kissed his cheek lightly. "Thanks," she murmured shyly, then took off on Sam's heels at a dead run, taking with her the essence of youth and promise.

A yawning emptiness filled Mike almost to the point of physical pain. He watched silently till they both disappeared into the trees, their light laughter hung in the air. Reassured that when the men showed up to eat, supper would be on the table, he scanned the cloudless winter sky for signs of the predicted ice storm. Nothing. Weatherman had blown it again.

Excited voices drifted toward him from the three men who'd spent the afternoon fishing.

He shook his head.

Even though Mike ran the fishing camp, he could never equate sitting in the middle of a frozen lake with fun. He'd tried, but freezing half to death while standing watch over what amounted to two crossed sticks just didn't cut it for him.

Adam and Doc, on the other hand, loved the sport and had even handcrafted their own tip-ups, as opposed to using the high-tech aluminum ones favored by Peppy and the rest. Doc claimed that when a fish grabbed his hook, his homemade red-flannel flags waved just a vigorously as Peppy's plastic iridescent orange ones. The debate had been going on for years.

Mike checked his watch. After all day on the lake, if Sam didn't provide a meal, they'd be ready to barbecue him. As for his new guest... She'd probably worked up a hardy appetite lolling around the cabin all day, protecting her salon-pampered skin from the elements.

Hamilton, give it up! Don't let her get to you.

She was here and he'd have to grin and bear it for a month. Bottom line? Her money would pay the bills as easily as anyone else's. But her disturbing presence went beyond her wealth, beyond her ability to resurrect memories of Ken, the accident and the lonely silence of the house without his brother's loud music and cheery voice.

Something about her roused the loneliness inside him. One look at her and he knew, gut deep, Jackie was not just another guest. On first sight, he'd sensed she possessed the knack of seeing too much with those startlingly blue eyes. Given the opportunity, those eyes would penetrate the darkest regions of his soul, regions that hadn't seen the light of day for five years.

Damn her eyes! They'd haunted him relentlessly all day. He'd spent his entire thirty-four years in the Adirondacks and as blue as the sky got, he'd never seen a shade that could compete with Jackie's eyes. They reminded him of a spring-fed mountain pool, misleadingly shallow and inviting—but, in reality, deep and treacherous.

The indignant expression she'd donned at his mocking gibe about valet parking stuck out in his memory. Along with all her expensive goodies, the lady had a fiery little temper. Although dangerous to his concentration, taming a woman with enough heat to start her own forest fire would be a welcome change from leaky roofs and missing cooks.

Laughter bubbled up inside of him and burst forth, startling him with its foreign sound. When was the last time he'd laughed? Really laughed? He couldn't recall. Had it been that long? Is that what his life had become?

His life. His life was Land's End, and he'd best remember that. The realization of his brother's dream had become his responsibility in the hospital the night of the accident. The night he'd come to say goodbye to his only relative—too late. He had to finish this for Ken, bring Land's End into its own, make it the success Ken had envisioned.

He allowed his gaze to run over the property comprising the fishing camp he and Ken had bought seven days after the U.S. Army had handed them both their discharge papers. Recently, however, Ken's dream had become Mike's nightmare.

Long stalks of brown grass stuck through the crusty snow, a guilt-ridden reminder to Mike of the landscaping cosmetics he'd let go in favor of a growing list of repairs. A molded cap of snow disguised the roof of a cabin in need of patching. Icicles masked in sparkling brilliance the gutter hanging askew from the cabin the men occupied—the men and Jacqueline Barrett.

The ice caught the sun and winked back at him, bringing to mind her diamond earrings and the image of her sitting cross-legged in the middle of the bed.

He cursed softly. The last time a woman had gotten under his skin this way, he'd been sprouting peach fuzz and wondering if he should buy a razor with his next allowance. He condemned his traitorous mind, strode from the boathouse, then headed toward the main lodge.

"Bless my soul. Would you look at that? Now ain't that a daisy?"

"What a beauty! Nice going!"

The shouts from the lake drew Mike's attention. Sitting on a camp stool next to the fishing hole in the ice where the men had shoveled away a circle of snow, one of the men held up a large fish for the others to admire. Mike smiled.

This particular group of fishermen held a special place in Mike's heart. Friends more than guests, they made him look forward every year to their stay from mid-October to mid-November. But so far this year, he hadn't had two minutes to sit and talk with them as he usually did. The emptiness inside him suddenly throbbed.

His decision made, Mike headed for the middle of the lake to check out the latest catch, the aching need for companionship outweighing the call of duty.

As he neared the group, he recognized Doc standing to one side, beaming like a new father, and Adam showing more animation than Mike ever recalled seeing in the normally subdued, retired teacher. However, the identity of the third fisherman escaped him. He could be Tommy, except he looked too small to be Doc's seventeen-year-old grandson.

When Mike had nearly reached the cleared area on the ice, the mystery man drew the bright orange knit cap from his head, allowing a cascade of blond curls to tumble down his back. The perfume he'd noted in the cabin earlier wafted toward him. Unlike Annie's, it conjured up erotic images of long hot nights and tangled sheets. Mike stopped dead in his tracks.

"Jackie?" Her name burst unbidden from his lips.

"Hey, Mike." Doc beckoned him closer with a wave of his hand. "Look who Jackie snagged. Old Silver Scales."

Mike recognized the name of the eighteen-inch fish purported to be the oldest and most cunning in Hidden Lake. The one Doc had been trying to catch for ten years. The old doctor's expression showed just a hint of disappointment.

Neither Doc nor the fish, however, held Mike's attention. He had eyes only for the woman who had turned toward him.

Her face glowed. A slight breeze whipped her hair, tossing it haphazardly across her wind-burned cheeks. A few stray hairs had worked loose of her barrette and had been captured in her long lashes. Excitement sparkled from her blue eyes.

Impulsively, he brushed the hair behind her ear. His fingertips tingled. Desire knifed through Mike's gut.

Jackie sobered and stiffened; the sparkle left her eyes. She drew away, as if repulsed by his touch.

Mike's nerves shrieked a warning. He withdrew mentally.

"Let's get this old reprobate in the creel before he takes it into his head to jump back down that hole." Adam handed Jackie a pair of pliers, then opened the wicker, flat-sided basket holding five other fish and placed it within her reach.

Jackie accepted the pliers, acutely aware of Mike's speculative appraisal, agitated that her face still bore the sensations generated by his casual touch.

He's clearly waiting for me to ask for help. Well, hell would freeze over first. This monster fish would have to open his mouth and swallow her like Jonah before she'd yell uncle.

Determination squarely in place, she slid her hand over the fish's head and down to grasp him firmly around his gills, or as firmly as one could grasp something weighing as much as a block of solid lead and as amiable as the fishing camp's owner.

Studiously ignoring the slime oozing between her fingers, she captured the hook's eye between the nose ends of the pliers. Squeezing hard, she twisted the barb to free it from the fish's bottom lip. The fish fought to free itself.

She bit her tongue and squeezed tighter, recounting in her mind Adam's admonition that fish don't have nerves in their mouth. The hook broke loose with a stomach-wrenching crunch. Swallowing repeatedly, she took a deep breath, then deposited her catch in the open creel Adam had set out for her.

Casting a smug glance at the man hovering nearby, she dipped her hand into the bait bucket's icy water. How she'd love to wipe that smirk from his gorgeous face. She quickly captured a small silver minnow, threaded it on her hook, dropped the baited hook back in the hole, then reset the spring-loaded arm holding the red flag on the tip-up.

"I'm impressed. You seem to have this fishing stuff down pat," Mike said, his tone hard to assess. Was he teasing or was he sincere?

Still smarting from their earlier encounter, she would have liked to believe the latter. The last thing she wanted was for this overbearing lumberjack to think he got to her in even the slightest way. Better she just ignore him completely, but ignoring a grizzly bear looming over her would have been easier.

"I'm trying." Despite her best efforts, her tone emerged unsteady. Never in her life had she been so strongly affected by a man's mere presence, but Mike pushed buttons she hadn't even known she possessed.

"She's doing just fine," Doc crowed. "And we only had to show her once."

"Shame," Mike interjected, eyeing the creel holding Jackie's prize catch. "You've been trying to hook him for a long time, Doc."

Jackie's penitent gaze flew to Doc. Her conscience bit down hard on her excitement.

Doc nodded solemnly. "Yup. 'Bout ten years." Then his round face brightened. He fingered his glasses back to the bridge of his nose. "Jackie did it her first time out."

"Beginner's luck." Mike dissected Jackie with what she read as an accusing gaze.

Obviously his good mood of a few moments ago was a lapse in sanity. They were back to being adversaries and she had no idea why.

Hell, she hadn't asked the stupid fish to bite on her hook. What did she have to do to please this man? Why she even bothered to try remained an even bigger mystery.

Doc frowned in Mike's direction. "Jackie's a natural." The older man favored her with a warming smile.

Bolstered by the pride ringing in Doc's voice, even if he had embroidered on her talents, Jackie stood. She hiked up her drooping pants, rolled the sleeve of Adam's jacket back, then, before it landed in the open hole, rescued a forgotten mitten. Had it not been for the "idiot" mittens being connected by the string threaded up one sleeve of her jacket, around her neck, then down the other sleeve, her mittens would have been fish food hours ago.

Mike observed her every move. As nonchalantly as she could, with her stomach doing a good imitation of Old Silver Scales trying to make good his escape from the basket, she shuffled her overlarge, borrowed boots to the small alcohol stove. Pouring herself a cup of coffee from the steaming pot and pretending to inhale the rich aroma, she kept a surreptitious eye on Mike. He picked up the creel, opened the lid, then peered at the collection of fish in the bottom of the basket.

"Looks like you've *all* had a good day. If you bring these up to the house, Sam'll clean them for tomorrow night's supper."

"Doc and I never wet a line." Adam pointed to the pile of tip-ups still tied together near the little stove. He stepped forward and placed a hand on Jackie's shoulder. She glanced over at her fishing buddy. His already abused nose glowed even brighter from wind and sunburn. "Jackie caught every blasted one of 'em. Doc and I have just been watching her haul 'em in."

"Amazing," Mike drawled.

Jackie tried to let his subtle mockery roll off her, but he wasn't making it easy. He didn't have to gush, but he could at least show a little enthusiasm for an accomplishment she viewed as nothing short of a miracle that, considering the vastness of the lake and the size of the hook, the fish had found her bait at all.

"Sure is," Adam went on as if nothing abnormal had transpired. "Like Doc said, this girl's a natural angler."

Jackie took silent pleasure in the surprised expression on Mike's face. The pompous air leaving his balloon was almost audible.

"I just did what you guys told me," she said, unable to eliminate the smugness from her tone completely.

"Hogwash!" Doc exclaimed. "You went at it like you'd been doing it all your life." He turned to face

Mike. "You'll have to ask Jackie what she wants to do with her catch."

She favored Doc with a smile, then turned to Mike. "If everyone's catch is usually cooked for supper, then by all means, take them."

He hesitated, closed the creel, then replaced it on the ice. "On second thought, since it's highly doubtful Jackie has spent her life fishing, maybe she'll want to take Old Silver Scales home and have him stuffed to hang in her trophy room." *Along with all the hearts she's no doubt got there.*

Shoving his hands in his pockets, he nodded to Doc and Adam, stared for a long moment at her, then turned and strode toward shore.

Jackie glared at his retreating back. What exactly had she done to this man to make him dislike her so much? His disposition would be serious competition for a...a... Frustrated anger hampered her thought process from supplying an acceptable comparison.

"Great idea," she finally called after him, knowing how childish she sounded, her strident tones echoing around the open lake. "*Stuffing* it is exactly what I had in mind!" She glared meaningfully at where Mike's jeans clung enticingly to his tight buns. "And the fish isn't the only thing I'd like to *hang*."

Mike glanced back at her.

Was he smiling? *Right, Jackie.* And tomorrow the Hudson River will become a tributary of the Nile.

Doc laughed and shook his head. He stretched his arms above his head, then grimaced in pain. Placing a palm against the small of his back, he smiled apologetically at Jackie and Adam. "Cold's beginning to seep into these old bones. You two about ready to call it a day?"

Throwing one more angry look in the direction Mike had gone, Jackie nodded. "I guess so."

She'd been enjoying herself for the first time in weeks, and now the fun seemed to have drained out of it—thanks to Mr. Congeniality. To think, when he'd come out on the lake, she'd been stupid enough to believe he'd buried the hatchet.

"You go on up, Doc. Jackie and I can bring our things along." Adam had already started to assemble the scattered evidence of their long day on the ice.

"Sure I can't help?" Doc hovered, glanced longingly at the creel holding Old Silver Scales, then rubbed his mittened hands together.

Although he'd tried to downplay it, Jackie had noticed Doc's movements had become a bit stiffer as the sun had lowered in the sky and the temperature had dropped. "We've got it covered. You go ahead. The boxes I haul around in the kitchen back home are bigger than anything here."

Both men stared at her quizzically.

Damn! She'd done it again. Good thing she'd never considered a job in the Secret Service. She flashed them a lopsided grin.

When both men seemed to dismiss her slip of the tongue with a shrug, she heaved a sigh of relief.

Adam continued to gather their belongings. Doc delayed his departure by observing his friend's movements. In turn, Jackie studied Doc, her conscience nagging her for more than one reason. She should have realized these men couldn't take the cold for as long as she. Guess she'd been having too good a time. However, Doc's continuing presence made it hard for her to forgive herself. Obviously, he wasn't going to move anytime soon.

"It's not getting any warmer. And your arthritis isn't getting any better, Doc. Get on back to the cabin and warm up," she ordered firmly. "Adam, hand me that creel, please. I want to take one more look at Old Silver Scales before he ends up as our supper."

Adam did as she asked, then scurried about getting the last of the fishing gear together. Jackie waited while Doc cast one more covetous peek at the creel, then ambled off, eventually disappearing into the thick trees edging the lake.

Opening the basket, Jackie extracted the slimy celebrity, then raised him to eye level. Ugly son of a gun. His shiny scales reminded her of crushed aluminum foil, and his glassy bulbous eye glared back at her accusingly. Just what she needed—one more judgmental male.

She stepped to the side, close to the hole in the ice, ostensibly to give Adam access to the bait bucket. Sending a glance at Adam's bent back, she loosened her hold on the fish. Sensing this newfound freedom, Old Silver Scales twisted once and slipped easily from her grasp. The fish hit the ice, did a half gainer onto its side, then, with a helpful nudge from the toe of her boot, slithered into the water and out of sight. Satisfaction curved her lips.

Adam jerked upright and stared at the empty hole. "Oh, Jackie! Oh, dear, what a shame!" He turned distressed eyes to her.

"Oops! Guess Doc'll have another chance at him, after all."

Adam's mouth quirked in a smile. "Nice."

"What *nice?* I just lost the catch of the year and you're saying it's *nice?* Clumsy is what it is. Just plain stupid clumsy."

"Stupid? Maybe. Clumsy...."

He studied her closely. Too closely.

Suspecting he might be on to her and before he could read the truth in her eyes, she quickly averted her face. Without volition, her gaze came to rest on the tracks Mike had left behind. She frowned at the shoreline.

I do have my moments, Hamilton. Contrary to pop-ular belief.

"Jackie?"

Rearranging her features, she pivoted toward Adam, who still looked skeptical.

"Did you do that intentionally?"

"Now that's the silliest question I've ever heard." She grabbed the creel from the ice and threw the strap over her shoulder. "Why would I let a prize like that get away on purpose?" Unwittingly, her gaze re-turned to the edge of the lake and the lone set of tracks leading toward the main lodge.

Adams's hand came to rest gently on Jackie's arm. "My wife used to say that whatever escapes today could always be caught tomorrow.'' He followed her gaze.

"What if it doesn't want to be caught?'' she asked, refraining from acknowledging they no longer were talking about Old Silver Scales.

"Some catches are worth the persistence it takes to land them.'' Adam picked up his share of the fishing gear and trudged across the snowy ice toward the cabin. The ice cracked and snapped ominously, but she'd learned it meant nothing, just the ice absorbing their weight, getting used to their presence. Maybe that's all Mike needed—a few days to get used to having her around.

As Jackie followed Adam off the ice, his words swirled in her head. She didn't want to catch Mike Hamilton any more than she'd wanted to catch Old Silver Scales.

Adam with his riddles and Doc with his talk of what Mike really needs had her thinking far too much. And she didn't want to think about Mike except maybe in terms of a strategically delivered swift kick. But this time her wise comeback didn't cut it. Against her will she found herself wondering exactly what Mike lacked.

Loaded down with a bait bucket, several tip-ups, a tackle box, a camp stove, and other items, they made their way slowly up the bank, then into the trees.

A few feet away, she could make out the tracks Mike had left earlier in the crusted snow. The man baffled her. Both times they'd met, with the exception of that one moment when he'd brushed her hair from her cheek, he'd managed to make her feel like a social outcast. Why? Did it have anything to do with this *need* of his Doc had spoke of?

Fingering her cheek, she looked around at the dilapidated state of the fishing camp.

Out of nowhere came an image of his disdainful appraisal of her luggage and the remarks he'd made about her car. That he needed money would be obvious to a blind man. Was that it? Did he envy her wealth? Is that why he treated her like so much.... She'd rather not put a name to it, even in her own mind. Ridiculous. Mike didn't impress her as the type to waste time on envy.

Lord, had it been Dave? Had he left his imprint here and now the backlash of another of his blunders had caught up with her? She shook her head. Were that the case, they wouldn't be so reluctant to talk about it.

Whatever had Mike's back up went a lot deeper. And she could easily make herself crazy just trying to untangle something she had no business getting involved with.

Just thinking about the satirical twist her life had taken brought a smile to her cold lips.

For the past two months, she'd done everything in her power to avoid declarations of undying love from men bent on getting their hands on her money. Suddenly, up popped a man who turned her knees to rubber with a glance, who angered her beyond reason, who shot shivers of fire through her with a single touch, and who couldn't run far enough or fast enough to escape her.

Go figure, she thought, trying to make light of a situation that had begun to take on an importance that scared her spitless.

book, and why it was there. Jan studied the text, smoothed its edges but...

On these, did the walls manage to pull a babble of some sort of reference to one of the important that organized until...

Chapter Three

Jackie glanced at the man, laden with fishing gear, who trudged along beside her in the snow. In the space of a few short hours, she'd become quite fond of both Adam and Doc. Their unconditional offer of friendship warmed her immeasurably, especially since Adam seemed to have cast himself in the role of her surrogate father, and considering the harrowing ordeal of the last few months, she could use a little TLC.

Until this very moment, she hadn't realized six months had passed since she'd last seen her beloved Florida-based parents, and that semiannual visits weren't enough to ward off the loneliness of separation and the constant reassurance of their presence and love.

"Have you been coming here long, Adam?" she asked, prompted more by the need to put mental distance between herself and the ghost of Mike Hamilton than by curiosity.

Adam paused. Setting down his burden, he drew a red bandana from his pocket with all the flourish of a matador. "Cussed cold," he mumbled.

Roughly, he swiped the handkerchief across his tortured nose, crammed it back in his pocket, then reclaimed the alcohol stove with an impatient gesture.

As they continued their trek back to the cabin, the crunch of their footsteps seemed to magnify and fill the corners of the wintery silence. A cold wind swirled around them, biting at their faces and pushing them to hasten their journey. So much time had passed since she'd asked her question that she'd begun to wonder if Adam planned on answering.

"I been coming here every year for the last ten years, since Irene passed away and I retired from teaching tenth-grade science," he finally said. His gazed remained riveted on the path. His lashes batted several times rapidly, as though to clear his vision.

"Funny how we all keep coming back year after year." He raised his head. With his moist gaze, he searched the wall of pines around them. "Most of us, except for Tony, Peppy and Tommy, don't do much serious fishing anymore." A thoughtful pause filled the silence. "I guess it's the company. Somebody to talk to, something to fill too many empty hours."

"Ever consider a part-time job?"

He hunched his shoulders. "Don't need the money. Besides, there's nothing I want to do. I loved teaching. If they won't let me do that anymore, then...."

His voice trailed off and Jackie felt a pang of sympathy for him. Why did society steal the life from its senior citizens with forced retirements? What would she do if someone told her she couldn't cook anymore? The idea went beyond comprehension.

"I tried retiring to Florida and taking up golf a few years back." He chuckled low in his throat.

"I found out real fast I wasn't going on any PGA tours. Spent more time in the water hazards and sand traps than on the fairway."

Jackie smiled, thinking of her father's daily pre-breakfast ritual of nine holes on the golf course outside the back door of the Florida condo he shared with her mother.

"I figured, if I was going to spend so much time in the sand and water, I might just as well be at the beach. Besides, the scenery's better there. All those bikinis." He glanced at Jackie, wiggled his bushy white eyebrows, then sent her a playful amber-eyed wink.

"Adam," she scolded gently, "I do believe there's a bit of a dirty old man in you."

His grin deepened. "That snow up there—" lacking a free hand, he arched his brows toward the abundant cap of salt-and-pepper hair beneath his red-and-black-plaid ear-lapper hat "—may look like the fire's gone out, but the flame still flickers from time to time." His expression grew solemn. "Then fall rolled around and I missed the changing seasons, so I headed back home to New York State."

Jackie stole another sidelong glance at her companion. Adam's humor really covered the loneliness of a man who who'd lost his soulmate, his purpose in life and, with them, his reason for living. She'd seen that loneliness often in the rheumy-eyed retirees who patronized Dave's restaurant.

"I'm starved," she announced, changing the subject deliberately. "How soon is supper?"

Adam checked his watch. "We'll have just enough time to get cleaned up and changed before we head up to the main lodge."

The main lodge. Mike. Another confrontation. Her shoulders sagged. Her pace slowed. Her appetite vanished.

AFTER EMPATHIZING with her on the escape of cunning Old Silver Scales, the men voted to let Jackie have the consolation prize of first crack at the bathroom.

Peppy expressed his opinion of incompetent women fishermen, grumbled his token protest about being done out of the bathroom, then lapsed into a brooding silence during which he helped Adam clean the fish. Tommy fell all over himself finding her soap and a clean towel. Rip slept through most of the discussion, and Tony endeavored to slip in an off-color remark, which Doc fielded with the ease of a professional baseball player. Harold, totally absorbed in the higher mathematics of divvying up expenses, missed the whole exchange.

Enchanted with her new companions, Jackie took advantage of a warm, soothing shower. By the time she emerged, she felt fortified, ready to face Mike again.

Despite promising herself she'd make no attempt to impress the owner of Land's End, she brushed her hair to a burnished gold and paid special attention to applying a light coat of ego-reinforcing makeup. Pairing a thick Irish-knit sweater with dark brown New Zealand wool slacks, she tugged on fur-lined boots and a brown jacket, then left the cabin to the men. As she walked up the hill toward the main lodge, she stuffed her long hair beneath a white angora hat, then hurriedly slipped her cold hands into soft matching mittens.

Lighthearted, she inhaled the cold air, then blew out a white puff of breath. Wrapping her arms around herself, she hugged close the peaceful night.

Stars winked from the ceiling of inky black, making the night sky appear like a darkened windowpane sprinkled with light-kissed raindrops. The only illumination, a full moon, painted sparkling silver trails across the newly fallen snow, sharpening the edges of the fir trees' blue shadows. The tantalizing odor of pine resin and wood smoke curling from the lodge's chimney perfumed the crisp, clear evening.

A haunting, expectant silence prevailed, broken only by the soft whoosh of her boots on the snow-powdered path. Somewhere in the distance an animal howled plaintively. A lone wild dog separated from the pack?

She listened for a repeat. But it wasn't the dog she heard. This new sound was different. Closer. She swung toward it and saw the silhouette of a man sitting on a rocky overlook at the edge of a small clearing. Instinct and her suddenly rapid pulse identified Mike Hamilton.

Curiosity winning out over good judgment, she

snatched off the telltale white hat and mittens, then stuffed them into her coat pocket. Quickly, she slipped into the purple shadow of a nearby tree. Her brain registered the absurdity of this game of hide-and-seek. Her pounding heart informed her this was no game.

Bathed in the brightness of the full moon's light, he resembled a stone statue. Cold and unapproachable. Still. Surrounded by life, but so still. Yet his sheepskin jacket, collar pulled high against the cold, and worn jeans, molded and stretched taut over thick thighs, proclaimed him to be all too human for her peace of mind.

Elbows propped on his spread knees, his fingers linked in front of him, he might have held everything near and dear to him sheltered in his palms, safe from harm, free from intrusion—protected.

For a long moment, she watched him. Something caught his attention. His spine stiffened in silent challenge to an unidentified adversary, reminding her of the wild dog's prey catching the scent of its predator. He listened, his whole body alert, shoulders squared, braced.

He shook his head. Dropping his gaze to the valley at his feet, he exhaled a long sigh.

Acceptance of the inevitable?

The wind played through his thick blue-black hair, ruffling it and curling the ends into the fur on his coat collar. He flexed his shoulders, then shifted his weight on the rock.

Impatience? Uncomfortable with himself? With life? With his thoughts?

Doc said Mike ran this place single-handed, except for Sam his cook and Annie his waitress. He had to be exhausted, about as exhausted as one man could get and still function, she imagined. Undoubtedly, nerves kept him going. Nerves and that stubborn determination she'd read in his eyes.

She began to reassess her resentment of him. Could his surly attitude be a product of frustrated exhaustion?

Raising his face to the sky, he froze in contemplation of the heavens for a long time.

Seeking answers? Seeking guidance? Seeking...what?

Perhaps the fulfillment of that mysterious need?

Her head swimming with unanswered questions and reminding herself that eavesdropping on private moments ranked right up there with peeking in windows, Jackie decided to make a quiet retreat.

Suddenly alert, Mike stood, then turned toward the wall of pines separating the clearing from the main lodge. Frozen in place, Jackie held her breath. So much for a clean getaway.

Staring fixedly at the trees, he waited.

Jackie waited with him, parental warnings from her childhood running rampant through her head. *Young lady, your curiosity is going to be the death of you.*

The trees rustled ominously. She prayed her parents' predictions weren't about to come to pass, and chanced a glance at Mike.

He slipped his hand slowly into the pocket of his jacket. The silence spun out between them, binding Jackie to the spot with invisible threads of reassuring serenity. Snow plopped softly to the ground.

The wind?

She glanced up at the pines, silhouetted motionless against the night sky.

A branch snapped. The reverberation ricocheted through the soundless night like a stray bullet. More snow fell.

The trees parted.

Jackie clamped a hand over her mouth to muffle her gasp of surprise.

Into the clearing stepped a full-grown, white-tailed deer. Mesmerized by this unexpected sight, she froze in silence to see what would happen.

The deer's bulky body, silvered in moonlight, moved with grace and precision, except for an almost imperceptible limp. An old injury, she decided, seeing no wound on his leg. A crown of antlers bearing at least a dozen points seemed to sway precariously atop his head, dwarfing Mike's six-feet-plus height. The animal's broad-muscled back quivered in waves from his neck to his tail, like a restless ocean current, bringing to mind an image of Mike's arms wielding the chain saw.

Afraid to move, afraid to even breathe, Jackie ventured a glance at Mike. Unlike her, though motionless, he waited, relaxed, knee bent, weight on one hip, while the magnificent buck made its way slowly across the clearing.

Grace. Beauty. Nature's power in a head-on confrontation with man's cunning.

And still Mike made no move.

The buck stopped a foot away from him, sniffed the air, twisted his neck as if to avoid impaling Mike on his antlers, dipped his head, then nuzzled Mike's side. When he didn't respond, the deer nudged Mike's shoulder, tipping him off balance. He chuckled softly, quickly regained his footing, then wrapped an arm around the deer's neck.

Jackie let out her trapped breath. Awestruck, she continued to watch the interplay between man and beast.

Mike murmured softly to the creature and drew his hand from his pocket, palm open. The deer buried his black nose in Mike's hand, raised his head, then chewed contentedly.

"So, Shag, you haven't deserted me. You're late tonight. Got a girl?"

The deer's ears flickered in response to Mike's soft voice. Shag finished chewing, then nuzzled Mike's hand for more.

"Take it easy on the sugar, my friend," he cautioned, giving the deer another lump. "You have to stay in shape for the next two months in order to outrun those hunters who want your head to decorate their mantels." Though light and teasing, his words held a mixture of sadness and anger.

Deep inside she understood his anxiety for his pet. No. His friend.

As if to prove her assumptions correct, Mike pressed his forehead against the buck's neck. "I can't lose you, too, Shag. Ken would never forgive me." His raised his head. The moon spotlighted his weary smile. "I have a way of losing things, you know. First Ken, and now..." His voice trailed off.

Shag raised his head, then brandished his antlers and pawed the ground, seemingly impatient with Mike's doubts concerning both his own ability to survive and the deer's.

A soft laugh issued from Mike, muffled by the deer's furry body. Patting Shag's black nose, Mike gazed into the buck's soft brown eyes.

"Yeah, I know. It's the same old story every time you come around. My trials and tribulations. Sorry, my friend. But it's your own fault. You shouldn't be such a good listener." He patted the broad neck. "You make the perfect confidant, you know. No fingers to point." He smoothed his hand over the deer's flank.

Jackie shivered, remembering the touch of Mike's fingers on her cold cheek.

Shag rubbed his muzzle against Mike's sleeve.

"Thanks." Mike stepped away a bit. "So, about this doe... Is she a likely prospect?"

Shag pranced in place, arched his neck, then snorted, blowing out great billows of white steam. Mike laughed softly.

"Just watch your back, old boy. Females have a

way of sneaking up on you when you aren't looking and scrambling your brains.''

Mike glanced over the deer's back, straight in Jackie's direction.

She moved back, taking sanctuary behind the tree trunk, held her breath and waited for Mike to confront her. Nothing. She leaned forward to venture a peek. Her boot slipped on a hidden patch of ice. She caught herself before she slid into view.

Shag started nervously. Pulling away from Mike, the deer stood perfectly still. His ears scanned side to side, like small radar antennae; his black nose quivered, testing the air for danger; his tail flicked back and forth.

"What is it? What do you smell?" Mike sniffed the air. "There's nothing there, old fella. Like always, it's just you and me."

A gust of cold air came from behind Jackie, swirling her hair across her face, blinding her to the man and the deer. She grabbed at it, pulling it loose just in time to see Shag bounding through the trees, his powerful back legs propelling him forward, his raised white tail signaling his alarm.

Mike's gaze remained fixed to the spot in the trees where the deer had disappeared. His face shrouded in regret and sadness. He exhaled a long, devitalized sigh. Her heart tightened painfully at the desolate echo of the ensuing silence.

"I'm sorry I frightened him away."

She hadn't meant to speak, to betray her presence.

Hadn't meant to let him know she'd witnessed this private moment between him and his friend.

The slow pivot that brought him to face her did not resemble a man caught unaware.

"You wear very distinctive perfume," he murmured. His low tone left the stillness of the night amazingly undisturbed.

His gaze locked on to hers.

Helplessly, she stared back into the depths of his coal-black eyes, searching his moonlit expression for a sign of the sarcasm, the arrogance, she'd come to expect from him. Both conspicuously missing. She started inwardly at what she did see. Loneliness. Vulnerability.

But before she could look deeper, he blinked, as if suddenly aware he'd allowed her to see too much. The curtain that protected him from the outside world effectively dropped into place. Had he wanted her to see another side of him, then for some reason changed his mind?

For the second time since coming to Land's End, this man wasn't bombarding her with contempt and ridicule. What had changed him? Not quite ready to accept this new Mike, she continued to hang back warily, searching for the answers in his closed expression.

He didn't look away. While she continued to try to appease this seemingly unquenchable thirst to just look at him, he stood motionless. Just as he had to keep from spooking Shag.

Ruggedly handsome, his features possessed a certain strength that would make him stand out in a crowd. Moonlight splashed shadows over his high cheekbones, probably a legacy from a long-forgotten Indian ancestor. His strong, square chin jutted out in silent defiance, proclaiming to all that he could move mountains simply by thinking about them, or did he just think he could?

Her gaze dropped to his lips. Lord, his lips. The urgent need to touch them, to learn their shape and texture careened through her. She breathed deep, knotted her fingers into fists at her sides and grappled for a coherent thought.

"He's a beautiful animal," she blurted.

"Beautiful."

"And surprisingly gentle."

"Looks are deceiving."

"Very true." *For all three of us, evidently,* she thought, sensing the conversation had ceased to be about Shag and hearing the thinly disguised warning in Mike's words.

"Underestimating the enemy can be dangerous."

Enemy? Is that how he sees me?

She opened her mouth to ask, but he took a step toward her, and words and thoughts crumbled into dust.

Then he rocked Jackie's senses. He smiled, genuinely smiled. Without disdain or mockery. Without the aloof crust he constantly hid behind. Nothing else could have unraveled her so completely.

Mindlessly, she watched his measured approach. A pine branch snapped beneath his boot. The sharp smell of fresh pine sap reacted on her aroused senses like an aphrodisiac. Desperately she floundered for some solid thought to latch on to in this sea of rocking emotions.

Christmas. She hadn't done an ounce of shopping...

He took another step. The flimsy thread of thought drifted away on the night air.

Less than three feet of space separated them. A slow, steady throb built at her core, then radiated to every part of her body. Defenseless against these foreign emotions taking over her logic, she reached for the solidity of the tree trunk. Anything to stabilize her reeling senses. Anything to anchor her in reality. Anything to stop the magnetism pulling her down into his velvety, brackish eyes.

Her knees wobbled, threatening to collapse. She sucked in oxygen, filling her nonfunctioning lungs with the biting cold night air. In the pit of her stomach, a fire began to flicker, grew with every second he stared at her, then burst forth into flames that threatened to consume her.

Another step brought him within inches of her.

He filled her vision.

His warm breath stroked her cold cheeks. The air between them crackled with awareness. Under his gaze, her lips tingled.

He was going to kiss her. And she was going to let him.

On a wave of sudden panic, she squeezed her eyes closed to free herself from his hypnotic spell. Moments later, she opened them slowly, then cautiously scanned the clearing.

Empty. Except for her and the tracks of a lone deer and one man, side by side, both bent on escape—the only proof the past few moments hadn't been the yearnings of her overwrought imagination.

Chapter Four

"Damn it to hell! It's not even noon and already the day's turning to crap!"

Mike tossed the scribbled note on the scarred oak cutting block in the center of the lodge's kitchen. Next to it, he dropped a paper bag. The bag split open like a ripe peach. Galvanized roofing nails slipped through the gaping hole in the side, then cascaded in a silver stream to the worn, cracked linoleum. *Murphy's Law.*

"So much for patching the roof."

In wry amusement, he gazed at the rapidly growing pile of nails, getting a perverse pleasure out of watching something he could stop, but didn't. His smile faded into a frown.

This day was certainly shaping up to be another winner. First, the ghost of Jackie had popped in and out of his head all morning, interfering with his work. Now, to make the day a total washout, he'd just found out that Sam and Annie had eloped last night and it was an hour before eight people would be expecting to eat breakfast.

"That is," he amended out loud, "if I can find someone in the next forty-five minutes to cook and serve it."

He scanned the tidy room and combed his fingers through his hair. Frustration ate at him. After he'd found them yesterday in the boat, he should have seen this coming.

Fighting the urge to hit something, he flopped down in the chair Sam used for periodic naps. *Had used*, Mike corrected. Distractedly, he watched the snow melt off the toe of his leather boot and drip to an ever-widening puddle on the floor, and he began to chuckle. This whole situation was straight out of a Laurel and Hardy movie.

"Mike?" Harold's quiet monotone penetrated Mike's thoughts.

A shock awaited the shy, retiring accountant. Eating constituted the one indulgence Harold prized above fishing and deciphering the unintelligible jargon of an IRS form. Anything threatening Harold's food supply sent him into an immediate tailspin.

Without explanation, Mike handed Harold the note, then went back to his contemplation of the nails. The last of the three pounds fell to the pile, slipped off, then rolled under the butcher's block, almost out of reach.

The wide-eyed gaze Harold threw at Mike bordered on panic. "This is catastrophic!" His evenly modulated baritone had risen at least an octave. "What'll we do?" Harold checked his watch. "It's almost time for breakfast. Who's going to cook it?"

Noting with little satisfaction that the older man had adopted the dilemma as his own, Mike glanced at him. "Damned if I know. Any ideas?"

Harold considered it for a moment, his salt-and-pepper eyebrows knitted together in a straight line, his lips pursed, his finger tapped thoughtfully on his chubby cheek. He looked as if he were in pain.

For a moment, the grimace deepened, then he brightened. "How about Jackie? She's a woman. All women know how to cook. It's in their DNA or something." He caressed the protuberance overlapping his belt buckle. "The Crosby women are all fine cooks."

Taking in the sixty-two-year-old bachelor's bulging middle, Mike took Harold's announcement as gospel, even if it bent low toward the chauvinistic side.

"Afraid DNA has nothing to do with cooking talents." If it did, Mike added silently, he'd have inherited some of his mother's, which he hadn't. "And I expect our newest guest would want to man this kitchen about as much as she'd want to trade her Gucci luggage and her little red Porsche for trash bags and a garbage truck."

As it had all morning, the thought of a moonlight-bathed Jackie brought images of her scurrying through his mind. Cheeks reddened by the cold. Hair tumbled into disarray by the wind. Eyes wide with fright, then trust, then...

For one scant moment they'd connected and she'd slipped under his guard, thawing a small corner of that frozen wasteland he called his heart. If he'd stuck around...

He blinked several times to clear the heady memories. Walking away last night sure as hell hadn't been satisfying, but it had been smart. He squared his shoulders in silent defense against his thoughts. At the moment, issues that didn't involve his libido needed his attention, such as how he planned to feed seven men and one woman in less than forty-five minutes.

Dragging his tired body from the chair, Mike snatched a bowl from the sink, squatted, then began scooping the nails into it. The letter from the bank in his pants pocket dug into his thigh. Brief and to the point, it summarily said, "Sorry, no second mortgage." If he didn't settle his financial difficulties soon, it wouldn't much matter who cooked.

"I guess until I can replace Sam, I'll have to man the kitchen."

"Can you?"

He considered Harold's question for a moment. "Sure. I'll call Tolley Sanders over at the Mountain Café and borrow one of his waitresses for a couple of days. She can take care of the serving and I'll take care of the kitchen."

Having taken a positive step toward solving the problem, he felt better. How hard could it be?

It wasn't as if he'd be cooking for an army. Just seven men and one woman. He'd keep it simple. Basically, he had no other alternative, except to send the men home with their registration money—money he'd already spent on lumber, nails and other materials.

Harold hunkered down next to Mike and held the bowl while he deposited the last of the runaway nails in it. "Well, that's certainly a relief. You never told me you could cook."

A flash of Ken's screwed-up expression after he'd tasted the spaghetti Mike had made their first night at Land's End brought a half smile to Mike's lips. Followed quickly by a wave of panic.

"Yeah. I guess you could say it's a little-known secret." Knowing in his gut he'd live to regret his lie, he rocked back on his heels, then cast a pleading look toward his companion. "Can we keep Sam's elopement and me taking over as chef between us?"

Harold nodded.

"Thanks. No sense upsetting everyone over nothing."

WHEN SHE ENTERED the cozy dining room Mike used to serve his small group of guests, food played no part in what Jackie had on her mind. Half of last night she'd tossed around the perplexing problem of the man she'd met on the overlook. The other half of the night, she'd told herself adamantly that she didn't care about that man, but she couldn't seem to get him out of her mind or to forget the smile he'd bestowed on her. That smile had been genuine. The look searing. The effect on her nothing short of an emotional earthquake. The thought of what might have happened if he'd stuck around for the aftershock caused her to shiver.

Sitting at the family-style table between the irascible Peppy, known also as Preston, and Rip, Jackie cleared Mike from her mind by checking out her fellow diners.

Across the table from her, Tommy surveyed her with the spacy gaze of a teenager experiencing the violent throes of his first crush. She made a mental note to do nothing he could interpret as encouraging. Young hearts were so fragile.

While they waited for breakfast, talk around the table ranged from fishing to Rip's latest Madison Avenue success, the very one that had driven him to the mountains to sleep off the drain on his energy. Harold cast longing glances at the closed kitchen door. Tony regaled his end of the table with a traveling salesman joke while Doc, whose real name turned out to be Jacob, shushed him and scowled in disapproval.

Adam intercepted Tommy's cow-eyed fascination with Jackie and endeavored to divert the boy's attention by explaining, in great detail, the intricacies of tying a trout fly. Periodically, Adam halted in his lecture and sent concerned frowns in Jackie's direction.

The kitchen door swung open and a pretty, redheaded girl in her late teens stepped through, a large aluminum tray balanced easily on her shoulder with the support of one hand propped under the center.

"Where's Annie?" The whisper swept around the table like ripples in a puddle, everyone but Harold disturbed by the absence of their usual waitress.

"Annie has taken some time off," the young girl explained, setting large platters of food on the table. "I'm Kim." She favored Tommy with a charming white-toothed smile, which, when the young man paid her only cursory attention in return, faded quickly.

"Breakfast is served, madam," Tommy said in his grownup, gallant tone.

He picked up the platter nearest him, then extended it to Jackie with a gawky flourish. Two eggs slid off and landed with a leaden plop on the white linen tablecloth. His ears blossomed with a flush of red that spread to his entire face. "Oops." He scooped the dripping whites and broken yolks onto his own plate, creating a stringy egg-white and gooey-yolk trail from the table to his plate.

Jackie hid her smile, pretending to be too busy helping herself from the platter to have seen. But one look at the white globs with yellow centers slipping to and fro in a pool of grease on the platter changed her mind. Giving Kim extra points for successfully transporting the eggs from the kitchen to the table without launching them into space, she pushed her plate back.

"I think I'll pass. I'm not very hungry this morning. Maybe I'll just have coffee."

By the time the platter holding long, dark brown strips of what might have been bacon made it to her, her culinary training kicked in. Even Tommy, who seemed to have a hollow leg to fill at every meal, wrinkled his nose and shoved his untouched plate aside. She could stand no more. As unobtrusively as possible, she slipped from her chair.

Tossing on her coat, she walked out the front door,

then made her way toward the back entrance to the kitchen.

Just as she stepped around the corner of the building, the door flew open and several blackened slabs sailed out, plunking down in the snow at her feet. The smell of burnt bread stung her nostrils. Toast? She kicked one lump of the charred remains out of her path with the toe of her boot, climbed the stairs to the back door, then reached for the handle.

The door opened again, and Mike stepped onto the porch, his red-and-black-plaid sleeves rolled up past his elbows, a white food-spattered apron tied around his middle. A green-and-white baseball cap, perched backward on his head, declared this to be The First Day of the Rest of My Life. Sobering thought.

Mike cooking? A grin tugged at her mouth. She fought it. If this was the first day of the rest of his life, his future looked pretty grim. "Problem?"

He took one look at her, pulled off the cap, pushed his fingers through his hair, snugged the cap back in place, then exhaled a long sigh and frowned. "Oh, hell. I might as well tell you so you can have your laugh and get it over with. Sam and Annie eloped last night. I couldn't find a cook to replace him, so I'm doing it." He cast a baleful glance at the charred bread. "As you can see, Julia Child isn't in any danger."

Recalling the many nights she'd been stranded without help in Dave's kitchen, Jackie could fully empathize. "Aren't there some local kids who could lend a hand until you can replace Sam?"

Mike threw her a surprised look, then squatted on the edge of the porch and grabbed a handful of snow. He formed it into a ball, then threw it at an old outdoor well. It hit the roof and shattered, leaving an uneven lump of white stuck to the dried-out wood. A shingle slithered from beneath it, then dropped to the ground beside a piece of toast, their appearances remarkably similar.

"Kids don't want to work for me for peanuts when they can get good money at the ski resorts over by White Face. Kim's on loan from Tolley's Mountain Café until I can at least find a girl to take Annie's place."

"Didn't they give you any notice?"

"Oh, sure. If I'd been reading the signs, I'd have seen this coming for a month or so." Mike picked up another handful of snow, shaped a second snowball, then threw it at the well, hitting another shingle. "Can't say I blame them." The shingle dropped off and landed atop the first with a soft thump.

"Oh?"

"I don't exactly pay to scale," he drawled. "And with only seven mouths to feed, they didn't need a tractor trailer to carry home their tips." He stood, inhaled deeply, and breathed out in resignation. "On top of that, the hours are lousy. How can two kids starting a marriage survive under those conditions? Wherever they are, they're better off."

"Maybe they are, but what about you? How can you do everything you do around here and cook, too?"

He cast a sidelong glance at her. Exhaustion and frustration lined his face. "If you've got a better idea, I'm listening." His voice emerged clipped.

Taking a deep breath, Jackie looked him straight in the eye and said a silent prayer that she wouldn't be sorry she let the lines of fatigue around those luminous eyes sway her good judgment. "I can cook."

Mike eyes widened with disbelief. "I beg your pardon?"

"I said, I can cook for you, if you want."

For the second time in as many days, Mike burst out laughing. He couldn't believe his ears. Ms. Barrett was offering to get her hands dirty in his kitchen. Right. And tomorrow the Pacific Ocean would be outside the front door of the lodge. But he couldn't ignore how good it felt to share his burden and have someone willing to at least listen. Too bad they both knew she'd never be able to make good on her offer.

"Thanks," he managed to say, touched more than he cared to admit by her attempt to help. However, the idea of Jackie in the kitchen had him leaning against the porch post, fighting down the amusement the idea gave rise to.

"Exactly what is so funny?"

"You," he choked, losing the battle to bring his merriment under tenuous control. "What's wrong with this picture?"

Her indignation written clearly all over her face, in the thin set of her mouth, the jut of her chin, the blue fire shooting from her eyes, Jackie glared at him. His laughter died. With her hackles raised, she was beautiful. No, beautiful didn't do it. Breathtaking.

"I *can* cook," she declared hotly.

"What? Petit fours? Finger sandwiches? Thanks anyway, but these men need substantial meals. That's what they paid for and that's what they'll get, even if I have to burn this place down to do it."

She stamped her foot in the snow, the muffled sound, he was certain, coming nowhere near to appeasing her anger. "Well, be my guest, Mr. Hamilton. You can burn this entire place down around your ears for all I care. Just do me a favor. Stand in the middle of it when you drop the match."

Mike stared at her stiff retreating back. What had he said to get her going this time? He'd just pointed out the obvious.

Damn! What a temper!

How all that sass fit into such a small body... Shaking his head and smiling, he turned back to the kitchen and the task of trying to produce one slice of bread that didn't resemble slab wood after a forest fire.

Dismissing Jackie's offer as the joke she'd surely meant it to be, he went through the door, his nose reacting to the roomful of smoke resulting from yet another batch of forgotten bread charred to a tinder. It might take him a day or two, but he was sure he'd get the hang of cooking.

If he didn't kill them all first.

MEN!

How had she ever felt pity for that insufferable pain

in the… Jackie stomped the clinging snow from her feet with unnecessary vigor and pushed open the cabin door. She glanced around the room. Deserted, except for the always prevalent odor of fish hanging in the air and Harold, who had again taken up the chore of dividing expenses. The long table in front of the fireplace was buried under an avalanche of paper. Where on earth did he find so much bookkeeping to do?

Hoping to go unnoticed, Jackie made her way quietly to the cordoned-off corner of the room that comprised her sleeping quarters.

"Can you cook?"

The words stopped her dead in her tracks. She couldn't believe that shy, retiring Harold had actually said something, and to her, of all people. She swung slowly toward him, combing her mind for an answer that wouldn't expose her secret. "Excuse me?"

"Can you cook?"

Jackie delayed her reply with a question. "Why?" *Atta girl, Jackie, baffle him with soul-searching questions.*

Harold leaned back in the straight chair and sighed. "Because if Mike keeps throwing together the same kind of meals he made today, we'll all starve by the end of the week."

Eyeing his rotund belly, Jackie hardly thought starvation a contingency Harold would have to face—even if she couldn't agree with him more about the caliber of Mike's meals. The mere memory of that morning's fare made her shudder. Then, remembering how Mike had laughed at her offer, she got angry all over again.

"Why are you asking me?" She stood back and folded her arms over her chest.

Harold rose, then approached her slowly. The firelight reflected off his bald head, giving it the appearance of a large, polished apple. "Because you're a woman."

Her arms dropped to her sides and she stiffened. She wasn't about to take any more putdowns from a man today. One a day was one over her quota. "And what exactly does being a woman have to do with anything?"

"God intended for the gentler sex to cook food for the men. You're a woman. So you must cook."

His sexist logic escaped her, but she quickly realized that coming from Harold, that would be considered a compliment and represented nothing more than his illogical assessment of life. Still, she remained wary about giving him a direct answer to his question.

Her averted gaze fell on the pale green pages of the ledger Harold had been working on when she arrived. In that split second, she came to a decision she'd been putting off for some time.

"Do you do accounting?"

His back came up like a challenged kitten. "I'm a Certified Public Accountant, Ms. Barrett. I have overseen the books of some of the biggest law firms in the State of New York."

"Are you any good?"

Harold puffed up like a bird drying its feathers, then took a step back as though her words would pollute his honesty and intelligence.

"Okay. Don't get all bent out of shape. I was just asking. I want to tell you something, but you have to swear you'll keep it just between you and me."

"Ms. Barrett..."

"Jackie."

"*Ms. Barrett*, my honesty and discretion have never been questioned. I view my clients' financial portfolios with the same confidentiality that a physician affords his patients."

Convinced, Jackie took his arm and led the portly little man to the table. "Sit down, Harold. I have a story to tell you."

"But the cooking," he sputtered.

"One thing at a time. First I want to tell you who I am." His eyebrows lifted questioningly. "Who I *really* am. Two months ago, I won the New York State lottery."

"My, my. How fortunate for you."

Obviously, Harold was not impressed. Jackie smiled. "I won the biggest lottery New York State has ever paid to one person."

"Oh, my." His bushy eyebrows elevated a good inch. His bowlike mouth fell open.

She had shocked the unshockable Harold.

"Let me explain to you what that means. It means if I should die tomorrow and go to hell, it can't be any worse than what I've been through in the past two months. You see, my dear brother, your friend

Dave, accidentally let my identity slip to the media. Since then, I have been besieged by all manner of nuts." She paused so he could digest what she'd told him.

"I came here to escape and sort out what I want to do with my winnings." She stood and began to pace. "My problem is, I can't even conceive of what I won, much less what to do with it."

Harold stroked his beard and nodded sagely. "Yes. I can see that would be a problem."

She spun toward him. "Problem? Problem? This is not just a problem. This is a replay of Napoleon's march on Moscow. And I'm Moscow."

Harold's mouth curled in a wry grin. "If memory serves, Moscow was the victor."

She frowned at him.

"What I want from you, Harold, is a list of investments. And, heaven forbid, not the kind that doubles my money. Can you do that for me?"

She flashed him a dazzling smile. It went right over his head.

"Depends."

"On what?" She hadn't had this much trouble since she'd tried to talk Mrs. Turner into ordering veal Oscar when she had her heart set on veal Parmesan.

"Do you cook?"

Back to square one.

"Harold, I graduated in the top ten of the class of 1988 at the Culinary Institute in Poughkeepsie and have been head chef at my brother's Woodstock, New

York, restaurant for the past four years. Does that qualify me?"

Harold looked as if he'd discovered the mother-lode. She could almost hear him salivating.

The imp in her made her add, "I won top honors for my chocolate bombe in country-wide competition last February."

"I...I...I..." He licked his lips and swallowed hard.

"Great! It's a deal, then. I'll cook us a meal here that'll make you think you died and woke up in gourmet heaven, my friend. You start ciphering."

Indignity had fallen back over his expression. He stood, then swelled his chest to its full volume. "Ms. Barrett, it hasn't been referred to as ciphering since the North beat the South at Gettysburg."

Couldn't prove it by her. She'd soon have at least some of the money worries off her shoulders, and that elated her.

"Why here?"

"Why here what?"

"Why are you going to cook here?" He gestured toward the seldom-used kitchenette. "Why not at the main lodge? Mike would let you use his kitchen."

Jackie frowned and took a step closer to Harold. The owner of Land's End would be about as happy to let her use his kitchen as he would be to make her Mrs. Mike Hamilton. For some nebulous reason, that thought saddened her. The cold air must have frozen her brain cells.

"Let's just say that Mike and I don't see eye-to-eye. For some reason that has so far eluded me, he doesn't like me. The farther I stay from him, the happier we'll all be.''

A thought occurred to her. Inviting Mike would be a great way for her to gain just a gram of comeuppance. How she'd enjoy seeing him eat crow along with his fish.

"Harold, why don't we invite Mike to dinner? After all, if you guys aren't there, he'll have to eat alone, not to mention cook for himself.'' The imp in her stretched and sighed in silent satisfaction just mouthing the words.

"Good idea! Not even Mike should have to eat his cooking.'' Harold placed a chubby hand on hers. "Mike's okay. He hasn't had it easy since his brother Ken died in that tragic car accident. Taking care of this place on his own has been rough.'' He sighed. "But someday, he'll find what he really needs.'' He winked at her, shocking her down to the soles of her feet. "And my guess is, he's getting closer every day.''

There it was again. In the space of two days, Jackie had heard three of the men allude to this mysterious need of Mike's. So far no one had offered to explain exactly what *it* was.

"And that is?''

A smile transformed Harold's pudgy face. Why, he looked almost angelic. However, when he summarily dismissed Jackie and went back to his calculator and ledger, there was nothing celestial about the speculative gleam in his eye.

Chapter Five

The large dining room outside the lodge's kitchen loomed dark and silent—and empty. On a round blue platter lay slabs of meat loaf. White congealed fat filled the crannies of its rough, blackened crust. The color reminded Mike of the toast he'd thrown away that morning, the toast even the birds had sense enough not to eat.

He glanced at the gracefully curved Seth Thomas clock resting atop the fieldstone fireplace mantel. Half an hour past suppertime. Where in hell were they? The food would be ruined if they didn't show up soon.

Casting a baleful glance at a bowl of peas whose wrinkled skins looked as if they belonged in a home for senior vegetables, he heaved a sigh of resignation. Time couldn't do any more damage to the food than he'd already done just by cooking it.

He walked to the window and pulled the drape aside. The bale of hay he'd left in the side yard for the wild animals now lay scattered under a dusting of fresh snow, but there was no sign of a human form anywhere.

Earlier that afternoon he'd seen all of the men head out toward town in two cars. Since then, there had been no sign of them. Could they have been in an accident? His stomach lurched. His gaze sought and found the telephone on the registration desk beyond the arched dining-room doorway. Were that the case, surely someone would have called. He knew that from…

Coming to a decision, he strode to the table, then snatched up the platter of meat loaf. While untying his apron with the other hand, he turned sideways, then pushed the kitchen door open with a well-placed hip.

"Take this to Tolley's hounds," he instructed Kim, thrusting the dish of ruined meat loaf at the surprised waitress. "Doesn't look like it's going to get eaten around here."

Seizing his coat off the hook by the door, he slipped his arms in the sleeves and turned to her. The acrid aroma of charred food and old grease clinging to the fabric drifted up to remind him of his culinary fiasco. "If you'd clean up the kitchen before you take off, I'd really appreciate it."

A bright smile broke out on her young face. "No problem, Mr. H."

"Thanks. I'll pay you extra for it."

"No need. I barely did enough tonight to earn my pay." She set the platter down on the butcher block.

"Mr. H?" Door open, Mike hesitated impatiently. "Where is everybody?"

Everybody translated to Tommy. Ever since breakfast, she'd asked Mike everything from the teenager's birthdate to his shoe size.

"Beats me, but I'm about to find out." He stepped onto the back porch, pulled the door shut, then bounded down the stairs toward the big cabin near the lake's edge.

JACKIE HANDED Tony a stack of paper plates, plastic silverware and paper napkins. "Better set the table. The food's about ready."

She glanced at the others lounging around the room, each having contributed his share of help, then leaving the rest to Tony and her.

Giving her a broad, lopsided grin, Tony took the stack of plates, then moved to the long table, which Harold had vacated quite willingly. "You really get off on this cooking jazz, don't you?"

Jackie thanked the heat of the small kitchenette for covering her flush. "It's...a hobby."

Her evasion didn't miss the truth by much. Cooking had been her passion since the first time she'd made cookies with her mother at the ripe old age of six. By the time she'd reached her early teens, she'd already set her sights on the Culinary Institute.

Cooking gave her a kind of satisfaction she received from little else. In her mind, the challenge of blending flavors and textures compared only to that of a rocket scientist watching a space shuttle lift off and knowing he contributed to the launch.

"Where you from? You live with Dave?" Tony folded a paper napkin and snuggled it up to the side of a paper plate sporting Bugs Bunny in a party hat. The store had a choice, the men had told her, of Bugs or Daffy.

"I have my own apartment in Kingston. Dave lives in Woodstock," she offered, carefully dancing around any specifics. "What about you? What part of New York City do you come from?"

Tony chuckled. "Guess it's not hard to tell I'm from the city, huh? Brooklyn. Lived there all my life."

Something in his tone drew her gaze from the head of lettuce she'd been carefully tearing into pieces for the salad.

He kept his gaze averted. "Bad place to raise a kid. Bad." When he glanced up at her, his devilish grin blossomed forth, but she noted the hint of pain lurking behind his humor. "Hey! Don't get me wrong. I had a great childhood. Who wouldn't in an Italian family? Always plenty of food and fights, but lots of love, too." He picked up a fork he'd just placed beside the right side of the plate, stared at it, then moved it to the left side, studied it for a moment, then moved it back to the right.

"Left," she coached softly.

Nodding, he moved it back to the left. "The Fresh Air Fund sending me to camp for two weeks is the part I remember best. Land's End reminds me of that place a lot." He paused thoughtfully. "Maybe that's why I keep coming back here."

Jackie made no comment.

"Yeah, well..." He waved away whatever thought had been troubling him. "I remember how I wanted everybody to come to camp with me the second year. The whole family. So they could see how beautiful the mountains and the trees are and get away from the crowds and the smells." He shrugged. "Of course, they couldn't. Only one kid from every family could go.

"Then I grew up and went to college. And here I am." He spread his arms wide and grinned that same pained grin. "A bartender with a psychology sheepskin gathering dust on a shelf in my bedroom."

Psychology? Tony?

How unique these men were. Each had such a different background. Each had his own reason for coming here, and only Doc's and Adam's seemed to encompass fishing. However, even they seemed to be more in search of companionship than sport. She hadn't talked to Peppy enough to find out what drove him, but she would bet her next lottery check that something very similar had.

"Well, I guess we're ready," she announced, pouring a creamy camp dressing over the salad.

Using a spoon and a fork as improvisational salad servers, she tossed the greens, then set the bowl beside a steaming platter of brown fish. Next to it a bowl of green string beans languished in a buttery garlic sauce. The aromas blended together to promise a mouth-watering meal.

"Cholesterol heaven," she quipped. "But since I couldn't talk you guys into a healthy meal, at least it's not burnt."

"Amen," Harold mumbled, holding out a chair for Jackie, then slipping into the prime seat directly in front of the platter of lemon-garnished fish. In no time, his plate groaned under the weight of his meal. He popped the first bite into his mouth, laid his fork down, rubbed his belly, then emitted a long sigh that bespoke pure ecstasy. "I've got something to show you later, Jackie," he said pointedly in a stage whisper.

She glanced at him and smiled, then nodded. *Thank goodness.* Soon she'd have the money worries off her mind. That would leave her free to relax and enjoy the rest of her month's vacation.

At that precise moment, a gust of freezing air blasted the room. Jackie looked toward the door and found herself staring into the very unhappy face of Mike Hamilton.

"Damn," Rip muttered. "I forgot to invite Mike."

Jackie gleaned a small measure of comfort from the fact that, so far, Mike hadn't picked her out as the target for his anger. He seemed to be leveling it at the entire group.

"Pull up a chair and join us, Mike." Tommy's enthusiastic invitation seemed to darken Mike's scowl.

"I suppose it never occurred to any of you to let me know I'd be cooking for nothing tonight."

Rip slipped lower in his chair and everyone else studied their plates.

"Sorry about that, Mike. *Someone* was supposed to invite you to join us." Doc lowered an admonishing glare at Rip, who slipped still farther down in his chair.

"And just who's going to pay for the food I'm sending to Tolley's hounds?"

"Poor dogs," Harold murmured, then shoveled a forkful of salad into his mouth.

"We will, of course. Harold, add that to our expenses," Doc instructed.

Harold nodded between bites of fish.

While the exchange between Doc and Harold had taken place, Mike came closer to the table. He checked out the food. His eyes widened. Making what appeared to be a conscious effort, he schooled his features, inhaled deeply and then licked his lips with the tip of his tongue.

Jackie's insides did a somersault. She nearly choked on a mouthful of fish and had to swallow several times to push it down her throat. Damn the man! No one had a right to be that sexy without even trying.

"So who's the cook?" Mike's gaze traveled around the table from one face to another, never reaching Jackie's.

The snub tweaked her pride. But at least he hadn't singled her out to be the recipient of his scowl. Their attitudes toward one another may have taken major strides last night, but after this morning, they seemed to be back on shaky ground.

Grinning and laying down his fork, Harold patted Jackie's shoulder. "Miss Barrett did the cooking. Seems she's—"

"Cooking's a hobby."

Harold glared at her, expressing without words his indignation at the fact that she thought he'd tell her secret. She smiled a weak apology.

"Hell of a hobby," Peppy put in, his normally disgruntled attitude replaced by a smile that rendered him very distinguished.

Jackie caught his eye and smiled her thanks. Peppy, his congenial side exposed, frowned and turned back to the business of acquiring thirds.

"Mike?" Tony had risen, set another place next to him, then got a squat redwood bench to serve as a seat. He held out his hand toward the setting directly across from Jackie. "Come on. *Mangia!* You won't be sorry." He paused for a second. "Of course, if you already ate…"

"No. No, I haven't eaten." Mike's gaze fixed on Jackie.

Lord, would he just park it? She nudged the platter of fried fillets toward the offered place setting. Her gaze remained on her plate, although her appetite had fled and she'd taken to rearranging her food rather than eating it. Absently, she squeezed a wedge of lemon over her fish. The pungent aroma acted like smelling salts on her floundering emotions.

"Which one is Old Silver Scales?" Mike asked, sliding into the empty seat.

Jackie froze.

"That wiley old devil got away," Adam said, throwing a conspiratorial smile at Jackie.

"Got away? But when I left you, you had him in the basket."

When Jackie looked up, it was directly into Mike's eyes. He waited for her to answer. She squirmed a fraction in her chair.

"I foolishly took him out of the creel to gloat over my good luck and got too close to the hole. He slipped out of my hands, and the rest is history." She shrugged, dismissing the subject and hoping he would be as easily duped as the others had when she told her tale.

He continued to hold her gaze with his.

A smile tugged at one corner of his mouth. A mere suggestion of the one from the night before—but just as lethal to her senses. Jackie grabbed the sides of the chair for stability. A merry twinkle brought his dark eyes to life.

Hells bells, he was on to her.

"Shame." His smile grew in both size and intensity. They might have been the only ones in the room, on the planet, in the universe.

"Yes," she managed weakly.

"What will you stuff and hang in your trophy room, now that your prize catch...got away?"

Expecting to see the light of sarcasm blot out the

humor in his gaze, Jackie caught her breath at the teasing glimmer in his eyes. Mike was teasing her?

His good mood infected her. She couldn't help returning his devilish grin. "I guess I'll have to find a replacement. Maybe I'll try for a moose this time."

Mike laid his fork on his plate, steepled his hands, then stared deep into her eyes over his fingertips. "I haven't a doubt that you would, nor that you wouldn't be successful," he said with a wink.

That small movement of his eyelid turned her body into a boneless lump, her mind into a wasteland.

Logs snapped in the fireplace. The rustle of paper napkins being crushed came from somewhere to her right. A chair squeaked with the restless movement of body weight. The aroma of garlic drifted up from her untouched plate. Still, the man across the table continued to hold her attention exclusively, while shoveling food into his mouth. How could he eat and not look at his plate?

"Not bad," he commented.

She'd settle for not bad. It far surpassed his earlier fit of laughter.

"Ahem!"

Peppy's throat clearing broke the spell. Jackie blinked and glanced around at the faces of the men, some grinning, some with averted gazes. She cast one more glance at Mike, who still stared at her. Slowly, she shoved her plate aside, wiped her mouth on her napkin, pushed her chair away from the table, then stood.

She didn't understand this change in him, and she

dearly wished he'd warned her it was coming so she could have prepared to ignore him.

"How about some music?" Tommy's high-pitched voice sifted through the maze of her confused emotions.

"Good idea, son." Doc flicked his glasses back in place, then pushed his bulk from the chair. "We'll clean up, Jackie. You sit."

"But I..."

She didn't want to sit. Sitting meant she'd have to put herself back in line with Mike's burning appraisal. Sitting through more of his scrutiny would be her undoing.

"No buts." Harold placed a gentle hand on her shoulder and guided her back into her chair. "It's the least we can do after the marvelous meal you just made for us."

Helplessly, Jackie resumed her seat. Avoiding Mike's gaze, she centered her attention on a tomato seed stuck to the paper tablecloth. The soft strains of a love ballad emanated from a large black boom box perched on a low table a few feet away.

Cautiously, she raised her gaze to the man across from her. Heavens, he was still looking at her. She searched her mind for intelligent conversation.

"Jackie, would you dance with me?"

She turned toward the voice. Tommy's boyish grin flashed at her from beneath hopeful eyes. His ears glowed like the taillights on a car.

Without looking back at Mike, she followed Tommy to the improvised dance floor the boy had created by shoving back the furniture. She'd have danced with the devil to escape Mike's scrutiny.

Mike followed Jackie with his gaze. She'd chosen a sky-blue sweater that hugged her shapely breasts, paired with a wool skirt of a darker shade that came mid-thigh. Navy stockings outlined the curves of her long legs. The first sight of her bared legs stole his breath.

When Tommy's arms snaked around her waist, Mike felt a tightening in his gut. Although it was foreign to him, he recognized the sensation for what it was—jealousy.

The idea jolted him. He couldn't believe he resented the attentions of an adolescent, who sported a crush big enough to launch a 747 and whose gangly body and its all-arms-and-legs appearance resembled that of a newborn fawn.

Tommy pulled Jackie closer, filling the empty foot of space she'd left between them. He guided her in an awkward version of a waltz. Jackie stumbled. Tommy caught her to him. Jackie pulled away, then stumbled again.

Mike smiled. The first misstep he could have passed off as clumsiness. However, had he not been admiring her legs, he might have missed the way she'd intentionally placed her toe behind her other foot, perpetuating the second occurrence.

Jackie put an arm's length between herself and Tommy, then glanced over her shoulder at Mike. She smiled. His heart tightened in his chest.

"Is Kim still up at the lodge?"

Confused, Mike nodded. "Yeah, why?"

Slipping from Tommy's embrace, she sidled up to the table. "Self-preservation," she mouthed, then headed off toward her sleeping quarters. When she emerged, she held the keys to her Porsche out to Tommy.

"You shouldn't be hanging around with us old folks." She jingled the car keys temptingly. "Why don't you use my car and take Kim to a movie?"

Tommy's eyes glowed. He looked at Mike. "Is she done working?"

Trying to suppress a grin, Mike nodded. "Should be. But you'd better hurry. She usually calls her brother to come get her."

The young boy needed no prodding. He took the offered keys, grabbed his jacket from his bed, then sprinted to the door. "Thanks, Jackie," he called over his shoulder, just before the door closed behind him.

"I hope all that enthusiasm isn't just for my car." Jackie slid into the chair beside Mike.

He couldn't believe how many of his preconceived notions about her lacked foundation. If, when she arrived, he hadn't seen the trappings of a rich woman, he'd have found it easy to accept Jackie as one of the working class. Even reminding himself that should Tommy damage the car, she could probably replace it five times over didn't dampen his admiration for what she'd just done.

"You are an amazing woman."

Her questioning gaze left the door and fell on Mike. The impact of her blue eyes made him take a deep breath. The exotic smell of her perfume had him struggling for solid ground.

She frowned, knitting her eyebrows together and creasing the smooth skin of her forehead. Mike balled his hands into fists, fighting the temptation to smooth the wrinkles marring her flawless skin.

"Tommy is in that half-man-half-boy stage. It's hard for him. He's still looking for his niche."

"Niche or no niche, that boy is sporting a crush on you the likes of which I've never seen. He's very vulnerable right now. And you handled him beautifully. Just like you handled Old Silver Scales's escape." He winked at her, and when she smiled back, the bottom dropped out of his stomach.

"I don't think it's any worse than any other kid his age has had on an older woman." She began pleating a paper napkin. "I'll bet, as a kid, you even had your share of crushes on older women."

He laid his hand over his heart and looked shocked. "Me?"

A broad grin traced across her face. His heart rate doubled. Exactly what in hell was he doing?

The last thing in this world Mike wanted or needed was to like this woman. However, it seemed a little late in the game to worry about that. Every time he looked at Jackie, something stronger than like, something that could easily lead to deeper emotions—dangerous emotions—reared its head. Emotions Mike seriously doubted he'd be able to handle.

Before he could form a reply, Doc's voice cut through his thoughts.

"If you'll give me the key to the lodge, we'll take the leftovers up to the big refrigerator."

In a daze, Mike replied, "It's open. I never lock my doors. Never saw a need to. Who's gonna sneak in? A bear?"

Doc picked up his bowl of beans and signaled the others that it was time to go. As their six companions, each commandeering a perishable item, marched single-file out the door, Mike and Jackie watched their desertion, helplessly. Tony, carrying a bulging trash bag and bringing up the rear, winked broadly and grinned lasciviously, then pulled the door shut behind him.

They were alone. Mike continued to stare at the door. If he shifted his gaze to the right, he'd encounter the woman who had the power to make his blood pound through his veins with a hunger for life that scared the hell out of him. If he looked to his left, he'd see seven beds, all beckoning to him with promises of cozy intimacy. In neither case could he find safety from his own fantasies.

A noise behind him drew his attention. Jackie had begun clearing up the remnants of the fish feast. He studied her movements. Graceful, sure, economical. Each time she performed a task, she accomplished it with ease, dexterity and precision. No wasted motions.

"If I didn't know better, I'd say you've done this before."

Her hand froze in midtask. She darted a look at him, then turned back to the pile of soiled paper plates, napkins and plastic silverware she'd carefully assembled. "I've worked at two or three charity functions."

"More than two or three, by the looks of it. Annie was the best waitress I've ever had and she didn't work with a fraction of the efficiency you do."

She shrugged and continued to work.

"And then there's the cooking. That's the best meal, to my knowledge, that's ever been served at Land's End. Why didn't you tell me you could cook like that?"

She turned slowly toward him, then arched an eyebrow.

"Okay." He held up his hands to stop any words she might decide to hurl at him in retaliation. "You tried. How was I to know you were serious? So how *did* you learn to cook like that?"

"I spent some time in the kitchen as a kid. Food preparation has always fascinated me."

Mike said nothing. Instead, he waited, hoping she'd keep talking. He liked the sound of her voice. It seemed to soothe away the trials of a day gone wrong.

But she said no more. Who could blame her? Ever since she'd arrived, he hadn't exactly encouraged her to make conversation. Why should she even feel he'd be interested in anything she had to say? So far, he'd doubted her and laughed at her. Not exactly encouragement for future conversations.

Well, there was no time like the present to remedy that.

"Jackie, I realize I haven't been the nicest guy

since you got here. I'd like to change that, if you're willing." He extended his hand. "Truce?"

A wave of warmth washed over Jackie, followed by the same alarm she'd experienced the night he'd approached her in the clearing. If she touched him, things would change. And she had the distinct feeling they'd change in a way that would alter her life even more than winning the lottery.

But she couldn't just stand there gathering dust. The man was making an effort to settle the mysterious conflict that had been going on between them.

As she saw it, she had two choices. Either she took his proffered hand and said goodbye to any peace of mind she still had left. Or she could straight out tell him that if she shook hands with him, the chances of her throwing him on one of the empty beds and ravaging his gorgeous body were very real.

As a weak alternative, she smiled. "Truce."

His eyes darkened. He took a step toward her. She froze on the spot, her gaze trapped by his, an emotional prisoner of her own runaway lust.

She really needed to get out more, to be with men more, so that when she was confronted with this kind of overpowering masculinity, this man who exuded sex appeal like most men sweat, she'd have a modicum of control.

His warm fingers captured her hand. Her senses came to life like the lights on a pinball machine. Warning bells clanged and sirens went off. But she held on to him.

Now she *was* in deep trouble.

She could see her reflection in his dark eyes. The totally ridiculous thought that she looked like a brainless idiot skipped through her mind. She tried to blink, but her eyelids, as rebellious as the rest of her body, refused to move.

"Maybe we should seal the bargain somehow." His voice ran over her like hot maple syrup.

Her vocal cords joined the body rebellion.

His gaze drifted over her face, then down to the spot where her heart kept trying to escape through her throat.

"Oh."

The word whispered from her in response to the feather-soft touch of his fingertips moving up the pulsing vein in the side of her neck. They moved across her jawline and over her chin to her mouth. Gently, he outlined her lips, then probed the moist opening with his fingertip.

Was this her? Was this Jackie Barrett, the woman who accepted any challenge, the woman who always had control of herself? The woman who desperately needed to think of something besides the sensations running rampant through her?

With superhuman effort, she managed to break her gaze away, only to discover that the room, too, had become a seducer. Golden firelight softened the shadows and emitted a warm glow that matched the one burning deep in her stomach. The intimate blanket of silence magnified the sound of her breath mingling with his. Even the evocative aroma of woodsmoke seemed to accost her senses like a Far Eastern aphrodisiac.

Her body swayed toward him. His head lowered slowly, hypnotically. When she felt his warm lips close over hers, she surrendered the battle and became a willing conquest.

Mike sensed her submission moments before her limbs yielded their stiffness and then melted against him. He tasted it in the compliance of her lips beneath his.

Sensations bombarded him so fast and so intensely that he couldn't trust his legs to support them, and he sat on the edge of the table. Jackie moved unresistantly into the V his thighs formed, their lips never breaking the seal.

Her mouth tasted tart from the lemon she'd eaten for supper. The flavor matched her feisty spirit, the spirit he'd come to respect and admire. Her perfume reminded him of clover blossoms, light, almost imperceptible. Her skin felt soft and silky. Everything about her invaded and saturated his good sense.

He lifted his mouth from hers. She mewed faintly in protest, so he framed her face with his hands and tasted her again. This time, he barely touched her lips, taking small samples of the passion she offered.

She wrapped her hand around the back of his head, threaded her fingers through his hair, then pulled him down into a deeper kiss, one that stirred his blood with excitement and sent it careening through his veins at breakneck speed. His body, already hard and ready, responded with a heavy, throbbing need where she nestled against him. He'd never craved a woman with such intensity. He'd surrender everything for one night with her.

Instead of the thought urging him on to take what she so sweetly offered with her inflaming kisses, it had an instant sobering effect. Mike pulled back. What in hell was he doing?

If he became involved with Jackie, he *would* give up everything. Everything he'd worked to preserve, everything Ken had dreamed of—Land's End. He needed his concentration for that and that alone. He had nothing to spare, nothing to be squandered on a relationship that had no future.

Grabbing his coat and slipping it on, he'd gotten halfway to the door before Jackie could marshal her thoughts. Dazed, she watched him grasp the latch and haul the door toward him.

"Jackie, I..." He dragged his fingers through his hair. "Damn it all, I never meant for this to happen."

Dimly she understood. She said nothing, acutely aware that she'd helped perpetrate this mistake, but also that he'd rejected her. That hurt unbelievably. Emotions clogged her throat, preventing a reply. She could only cling to the back of a chair for support and try to make sense of a world suddenly gone crazy.

"Damn it! Say something. Don't just stand there looking like an injured puppy."

"What's there to say?" she asked.

He looked more tired than when he'd come searching for his missing diners. The lines around his mouth had deepened. If she lied and said it hadn't affected her at all, she might be able to spare him more anguish. But she couldn't. "Did I like it? You bet your socks I did. I'd be telling a blatant lie if I claimed otherwise. Should it have happened? Sometimes that choice is removed from our hands. But no, it probably shouldn't have. Will it happen again?" She looked deep into his eyes and spoke as honestly as she knew how. "That's up to you."

Never in her life had she opened her heart so completely to another human being. Knowing how vulnerable it made her, all she could do was wait for the killing blow.

To her surprise, Mike laughed. "I guess I asked for that. But it would have been a whole lot easier if you'd lied." He closed the door, then took a step toward her. His hands came up as if to touch her, then he crammed them into the jacket pockets. "If honesty is going to be the policy, I guess I can go along with it. I owe you that much." His velvety gaze held hers for a long moment, as if he searched for the best words.

"I've never enjoyed a kiss more than I did that one. And you're right, we don't always have the option to choose who will and who won't..."

"Curl our toes?"

He revived some of the emotions she'd fought to tamp down with his lopsided grin.

"Curl our toes." Again, he seemed to struggle for words. "If it's up to me whether it'll happen again, the answer is it can't."

Jackie's insides plummeted. "Why?" The word

barely disturbed the uncomfortable silence hanging between them.

"Jackie, look around you." He yanked his hand out of his pocket and swept the room. "This is all I have, all I can offer a woman. Look at you." And he did, burning her from head to toe with his hot gaze. "I can't compete with your world. I have nothing to give any woman, much less one like you."

"I haven't asked for anything."

"No." He turned back to the door. "But you will. And whatever it is, I don't have it." The heavy door creaked as he pulled it open and a cold blast of air swept the fire's warmth from the room and from Jackie. "By the way, that was a hell of a meal you cooked tonight, and, if your offer to cook for me still stands, I'll hold you to it."

She stared at his back for a long time. Why did she feel she had to prove anything more to him? This wasn't her problem. She came very close to reneging, but then she recalled the lines of exhaustion in his face. Knowing she might live to regret her act of sympathy, she nodded, even though he couldn't see her. "It's still good."

Glancing over his shoulder, he flashed a weak version of the smile that had filled her dreams. "Thanks." For a moment he stared. "See you in the morning."

"See you," she whispered to the empty room.

Spotting his glove lying on the floor where it had fallen from his pocket, she grabbed it and dashed onto the porch, but he was already out of sight. She clutched it close, inhaling the now-familiar scent of him and the faint odors from it having hung in the kitchen, then walked slowly back into the cabin and closed the door.

With a heavy sigh, she leaned against the closed door. Maybe working in the kitchen was a blessing in disguise. Maybe by working where she'd have a chance to see more of Mike, she would come to understand what made him tick. Maybe she could find out why he scowled at her one minute, then kissed her senseless the next.

Pushing away from the wooden panel, she placed the glove on the shelf beside the door where she'd be sure to see it in the morning.

Cooking for Mike might be a godsend, in more ways than one. She slipped out of her clothes and into her flannel pajamas. This lady-of-the-manor lifestyle didn't do it for her. A normal day for her included productivity, not lounging around a hole in the ice. If she wasn't careful, she could easily go home an overweight millionaire.

Although meant to lighten her mood, her thoughts missed the mark entirely. No matter how much she attempted to rationalize away her reasons to cook for Mike, in her heart of hearts, she knew the real reasons stemmed from the fact that her out-of-control emotions had gotten her in way over her head. Any arguments that she had no interest in the rugged, handsome owner of Land's End were barefaced lies.

Chapter Six

Mike planted a firm hand against the kitchen door and pushed it open wide. He stepped to the side for Jackie to get her first look at the place she would be spending a good deal of her time in the coming days until he found a cook.

"Oh, no!" Before she could stop them, the words had slipped from her gaping mouth. She'd been expecting rustic, even outdated. Eclectically ancient had never crossed her mind.

Wide-eyed, she allowed her gaze to drift around the room. The only natural light source, a small, dusty window over a metal sink set in an unpainted square of plywood, did little to enhance the furnishings. Jackie leaned against a butcher-block table in the center of the room to steady the shock waves coursing through her.

"I take it, it's not quite what you expected," Mike said from near the door.

His voice drew her attention away from the kitchen and to its owner. His relaxed stance siphoned the strength from her body. Denim clad legs crossed at

the ankles, arms clasped across his chest, dark eyes—
deepened by his brown wool shirt—glimmering in
amusement, hair in slight disarray from the wind, he
looked sexier than any man had a right to.

Why couldn't he be short, fat and bowlegged?

Jackie averted her gaze and blinked several times
to clear his disturbing image. "Uh..." She searched
for words to describe the first kitchen she'd ever seen
that boasted a combination gas and wood stove.
"It's...quaint."

"Quaint. Now that's a description I've never heard
for it."

Mike advanced on her, then reached above her
head to pull the chain on the light fixture suspended
from an electrical chord hanging out of the ceiling.
The bare bulb screwed into a gizmo with outlet slots
to add other electrical plugs.

"It could use a few renovations and a little mod-
ernization," he said, pulling the chain and splashing
light over the kitchen.

Jackie rolled her eyes and scanned the room with
renewed horror. Demolition would have been her
choice. "So where's the microwave?"

"Still in the store is my guess." He leaned a slim
hip against the butcher block and joined her in her
appraisal of the room. "We haven't graduated to
those newfangled things," he said with a country accent.

A groan of despair issued from Jackie. She wandered to the refrigerator, a wide, wood-covered con-
traption with two doors. *I wonder where they put the*

block of ice, she thought, opening the door and surveying the remains of last night's fish fry.

"Aw, come on. Where's your sense of adventure? Just think what a challenge it'll be to cook in this place."

Jackie pivoted to face him. "Is that how *you* saw it? A challenge?" She could tell by his sobering expression that his own catastrophic run-in with the kitchen was trotting through his memory. "Have you ever given any thought to modernizing it?"

"Oh, sure. I've given plenty of thought to it. The problem is, there isn't any money to put the thought into action." He strolled to the only modern-looking cabinet in the room and caressed the lustrous oak as if it were alive.

She was transfixed by his casual gesture. An involuntary shiver danced over her skin, as if he caressed her and not the wood.

For crying out loud, he's discussing woodworking, not lovemaking. Get a life, girl!

"Ken built this. The whole room was going to be full of cabinets just like this. Along with one of those fancy side-by-side refrigerators, a dishwasher and a commercial stove."

"And?"

He swung toward her. The light in his eyes had died. "Ken never finished it. He had a way of starting things and then losing interest before they were done. He started this particular project the week before he died. I never got back to it."

Just how often had he been the one to finish Ken's projects? she wondered.

She came to him and laid her hand on his arm. "I'm sorry."

Mike jumped and removed his arm from beneath her hand. No one had verbally expressed sorrow at his brother's death. The seven men had tried, but none of them could get past patting him on the shoulder. The sympathy had been evident in their gestures, but until this moment, he'd never realized just how much he needed to actually hear the words. His mental burden lightened.

Maybe that's why he couldn't get past his anger at the woman who'd been driving the car. He'd never even gotten a pat on the shoulder from her.

He glanced at Jackie. Had that been the root of the antagonism he'd felt for her when they met? Had he been holding Jackie somehow responsible for Ken's death just because she had money?

Slipping out of her red parka, Jackie hung it on one of the pegs near the back door. She rolled the sleeves of her blue silk blouse to her elbows, then grabbed the white apron laying folded on the edge of the sink. Tying it around her middle, she glanced at her watch, then placed her hands on her hips and looked around her, obviously avoiding eye contact with him.

"Well, I guess I'd better find my way around and start breakfast before the guys show up and lynch me because there's no food ready."

Mike couldn't take his eyes off her. Her blouse, an obviously expensive creation that she seemed as casual about soiling as she would have one from the local discount store, pulled tight across her breasts under the apron bib. Her designer jeans molded her little tush just right. She'd swept her hair back in a ponytail to get it out of her way, leaving her profile clear and uncluttered, except for the few rebellious tendrils that had escaped the bright blue plastic clip. Although he could see the fine line of her cheeks and jaw, he much preferred her hair down, framing her face in sunlight.

The tightening in his groin told him he was playing with fire and had better make a quick retreat before things escalated out of control again. So why didn't he? Why didn't he just turn away and get the hell out of here?

"I've got some chores that need doing. By the way, Tolley needed Kim today, so she won't be in. I'll be back in a half hour or so to give you a hand." Easing away, he turned the knob, then, as he buttoned his coat, nudged the door open with the toe of his boot. He lingered in the open doorway, reluctant to leave her. "Jackie?" She glanced at him. "Thanks again for saving my butt."

She flashed one of those smiles of hers that dropped the bottom out of his stomach, then nodded. "No problem."

He swallowed hard. "Good luck."

Luck? To work in this kitchen of horrors it would take more than luck. It'd take a flaming miracle.

She pushed from her mind what Mike had divulged about his brother and walked around the room, familiarizing herself with the placement of the pots and pans. She had her own brand of trouble to contend with, and he'd made it abundantly clear last night exactly how he wanted their relationship to stay— distant, but friendly, and very impersonal. That meant his problems were his and hers were hers. And that suited her just fine.

And her immediate problem entailed cooking a decent breakfast for seven hungry men, and doing it in the crudest conditions imaginable. She pulled open the refrigerator door. Today she'd keep things simple. Until she learned her way around this place, simple would make the whole experience much easier.

Eggs, bacon, toast, coffee and juice. Couldn't get simpler than that.

On the bottom shelf of the refrigerator, bacon strips had been laid out on a large cookie sheet. She pulled it out and grimaced. One side had frost on it, the other was greasy and limp. This, she decided, had all the earmarks of becoming the longest day of her life.

HAVING STRUGGLED through a simple breakfast and a lunch of homemade soup and hearty sandwiches, Jackie now faced the challenge of cooking her first big meal in this culinary nightmare of a kitchen.

Setting the chocolate pie on the butcher's block, she marveled that she'd managed to get through baking it with only a modicum of problems—namely, a gas stove with only two working burners, and an oven missing the temperature-regulator knob. When Mike said *challenge*, he hadn't been lying.

Speaking of challenges, she recalled how the old coffee urn hadn't produced coffee until almost a half an hour past breakfast. Before she even started the preparations for the evening meal, she decided to get a jump on that fossil.

Lugging the water-filled urn to the side table, she filled the basket with coffee, then secured the lid. While dreaming of her brother's automatic Bunn coffeemaker at the restaurant, she grabbed the appliance's electrical cord. With the help of a metal step stool to boost her height, she captured the swaying lightbulb and jammed the plug into the slots.

An electric shock stabbed her fingertips, raced down her arm, then straight to her toes. She yelped and pulled away, losing her precarious balance on the stool and then falling backwards onto the butcher's block. Her tush landed with a soft squish in the center of the pie.

Just when it seemed her day had sunk to an all-time low, the door opened and Mike strode in. Of all the luck! Well, she'd just sit here quietly and wait for him to have his laugh.

His back to her, he slipped out of his down vest, then looped the sleeve hole over one of the empty pegs beside the door.

"I'm starved. You got any leftovers from lunch?"

Still peeved because his promised half-hour return had never occurred and because she'd spent too much time sneaking peeks out the window, imagining what might have happened to him, Jackie felt it prudent to remain silent. Besides, with her hand still tingling and her butt marinating in chocolate pudding, Miss Congeniality she wasn't. Instead, she rubbed her electrified fingertips, ignored the dampness leaching through the seat of her jeans and glared at his back, content to wait for the inevitable when he got his first good look at her predicament.

Mike pivoted toward her, then stopped dead. His gaze wandered over her to the metal step stool, then to the coffee urn. Having the unmitigated gall to grin at her, he added insult to injury by breaking out in unbridled laughter.

What a charming picture she must have presented with chocolate pudding oozing from beneath and her hair no doubt standing on end from the electrical charge. The mental picture she painted of herself made her fight to keep from smiling. He wasn't getting off that easily.

"I forgot to warn you," he said around hoots of mirth, "that outlet bites. And if, by any chance, you were standing on that step stool, you really put your foot in it."

Jackie continued to glare, her amusement dimming slightly with every snicker from this man who had the knack of bringing her temper to a boil as fast as he could her blood. Slipping off the butcher's block, she peeled the pie plate from her rump.

"My foot isn't what ended up in it," she said through clenched teeth.

"That's a unique way to serve dessert, but I'd recommend dessert plates from now on."

Casting one more burning look at his grinning face,

she turned away to put the pie plate on the sink's drain board. "I'll remember to include that in the 'How to Set an Elegant Table' section of my first cookbook."

Muffled noises signaling a new fit of laughter bubbling from Mike came from behind her.

With his hand clamped tightly over his mouth to silence the mirth he knew had to be getting to Jackie but that he was unable to curb, he sauntered to the refrigerator and opened the door. Stealing a cherry tomato from a basket on the shelf, he popped it into his mouth.

Just then, something cold, wet and slimy hit him in the back of the head, then slid down his hair and into his shirt collar.

Slowly, he turned to face Jackie. She'd been irritated as hell when he'd first come in, but he couldn't believe she'd actually throw something at him.

Standing at the sink, a wicked grin painting her lips, she licked chocolate pudding from her fingers. For a long moment, he watched her, his groin tightening with every swipe of her pink tongue. So, she wanted to play, did she?

From inside him rose joyful anticipation, a feeling he hadn't experienced since he'd passed up the bubble-gum counter for a condom display. He approached her slowly and deliberately.

Smirking, she backed up, her blue eyes dancing. Her retreat stopped short when her legs came up against the solid butcher's block.

"Careful, Hamilton. Don't do anything you'll regret. I'll be forced to retaliate." A bubble of laughter erupted from her.

Stopping a few inches away from her, he parted his lips slightly and chomped down on the tomato. A spray of seeds, pulp and juice, shot out, painting the front of Jackie's blouse.

"Gotcha!"

She raised her gaze to his, her grin still in place and a devilish light sparkling in the depths of her eyes.

Not sure of her next move, Mike backed up a step.

She followed, looking intently at his lips. Walking her fingers up his shirtfront, she circled her hand around his neck. His heart pounded. His groin tightened. He allowed the pressure of her hand to pull his mouth toward her upturned lips. His eyes closed in anticipation of the kiss.

Just as her warm breath brushed his lips, she moved her hand and ground the pudding inside his collar into this neck. Before he could grab her, she ducked beneath his arm, stationing herself with the butcher block between them.

"I was the food-fight champ in college, fella." She did a little dance, like a prizefighter warming up for a match. "You're messing with a master of the game."

"Master, huh? We'll see who's the master here."

Sticking out her chin, she tapped it with the tip of her finger. "Come on, big boy, give it your best shot."

Continuing to bob and weave, she took little forays

to his side of the block, teasing him, tempting him. When he made no move to go after her, she paused, hands on hips. "You aren't surrendering already, are you? I just got started."

"Give up? Fat chance, Barrett." He'd had more fun in the past few minutes than he'd had in years. And it felt good. Damn good.

"Come on," she taunted, pouting her lips playfully. "Let your hair down, Hamilton. Show me what you've got."

Mike inhaled sharply. "Lady, you're playing with fire. If you're not real careful, you could get burnt."

"You gotta catch me first." She put her hands back on her hips, daring him to carry out his threat.

God, but she was gorgeous, even with tomato seeds peppering her blouse. Life fairly jumped from her eyes. A line of white teeth showed through her impish grin. The heat of the kitchen glowed in her cheeks. Scattered wisps of honey gold hair framed her face. The top three buttons of her blouse were open, revealing the beginnings of her deep cleavage with every breath she took.

Pudding ran down his back, but he ignored it, unable to take his gaze off her. He put out a hand to steady himself and felt pudding ooze between his fingers. With perfect aim and no warning, he scooped up a handful and threw it at her.

The pudding hit her chin, dripped off, landed on her collarbone and then slid slowly out of sight beneath the material of her blouse.

"Bull's-eye!"

"Now you've—" the pudding skidded into her bra, then slithered over her breast; the erotic sensation stole her words "—done it," she finally whispered.

She could have saved her breath. No one was listening. Mike seemed transfixed by the spot on her chest where the material had begun to dampen and cling.

Food fights came with the territory at a culinary school, and she'd engaged in her share, but none of them had ever turned sensual.

The room had become suddenly quiet. The only sound was the steady groan and gurgle of the old urn churning out a pot of that horrible black stuff the men laughingly referred to as coffee.

Mike pinned her with his velvet gaze. Her labored breathing ceased completely. He walked slowly toward her. Stopping directly in front of her, he bent, then gently laved the pudding from her chin. Slowly, deliberately, his gaze tightly focused on hers, he licked his fingers.

Sensations not unlike the shocks she'd received from the coffeepot whirled through her body, sparked her nerve endings, then ignited a fire in her lower belly.

"Best dessert I've had in ages." His voice had taken on a low and silky quality.

He perched on the edge of the butcher block and pulled her against him. Like a zombie, her body obeyed his commands. While he loosened the clip holding her ponytail in place, she stood as if in a trance. Her hair cascaded down around her cheeks, skimming over her sensitized skin.

As he assessed her reaction, he folded the sides of the blouse back to reveal the remains of the pudding coating her half-exposed collarbone.

He lowered his gaze. "And the serving dish is sensational. Seconds," he murmured before lowering his head and laving the sweet treat from her skin.

Her knees buckled. She leaned into him. Although she was barely conscious of her movements, her hands came up to cradle the back of his head, shamelessly drawing him closer. A faint moan escaped from her lips. She grasped his shoulders to steady her trembling body. The room tilted.

This was crazy! One of the men could walk in at any minute. If Mike didn't stop, God help her, she'd have to make the effort.

"I thought you said this couldn't happen again," she breathed between efforts to drag much-needed air into her burning lungs.

Mike raised his head, his hands resting on her rib cage, his thumbs grazing the underside of her breasts. "I said we couldn't kiss again."

"Oh."

"In case you haven't noticed, I haven't kissed you." His gaze dropped to her lips. She licked them. He closed his eyes for a second, then opened them. "But I can always break my word."

His deep velvety voice slid over her like liquid satin, touching her everywhere, slipping into every part of her, saturating her mind. Even the roof of her mouth tingled.

"Oh."

He grinned. "That's what I like. A woman who can express herself."

Helplessly, she licked her lips again.

"I warned you."

His head lowered and he covered her mouth. He tasted like chocolate pudding. He tasted like tomorrow and the day after and the day after that—like forever. Her bones turned to mush. She leaned into his chest and wrapped her arms around his neck.

The kitchen door creaked. They sprang apart like two guilty teenagers caught by their parents. Mike stopped her long enough to pull her blouse together. They turned simultaneously to face Peppy's wide grin.

"Ah...I just stopped in to tell you that we won't be here for supper. There's a good football game on TV tonight, and everyone's meeting at Tolley's to watch it on the big screen. He's putting out a big buffet." Peppy's gaze took in the dark splotches of pudding on her blouse and Mike's tousled hair.

Heat rose in Jackie's cheeks. She nodded dumbly.

Knowingly, Peppy looked from one to the other. "Well, don't let me interrupt. You two just finish what you were doing." He flashed them another grin, then pulled the door shut behind him.

Conscious that she was avoiding eye contact with him, Mike watched as Jackie slipped around the table to the sink, turned on the faucet, then made a concentrated effort to rinse the pudding from her cleavage. He studied her back. Thank God for Peppy's interruption. If things had progressed any farther, no telling what would have happened.

What would have happened, my friend, is that you'd have hauled her upstairs to your room. Then you'd have spent the night making love to her.

And how exactly did he feel about making love to Jackie?

Just the thought sent his blood singing through his veins like a current through a high-tension wire. Holding her naked body next to his and losing himself in her would be like dying and being reborn, an experience that would change him forever.

He glanced at her once more, grabbed his vest off the peg, tucked his arms into the sleeve holes, then ducked out the door.

It had started to snow. The delicate, sparkling, white flakes caught the faint light from the kitchen, turning the grounds into a diamond mine of iridescent gems all glimmering and transforming the dilapidated camp into a beautiful fairyland.

He stepped off the porch, then turned his face skyward. The gently falling snow cooled his overheated flesh, but the fire inside that Jackie had ignited burned bright and strong.

Chapter Seven

After a near-sleepless night, Jackie had come to one hard conclusion. She'd fallen in love with Mike. Where and how eluded her, but love it had to be. Why else could the man turn her into a giddy teenager and erase all rational, sensible thought from her mind with a look? And what he could do to her physically, she didn't even want to think about.

When had it happened? Maybe when he rescued the bird's nest that first day. Maybe the night with the deer on the lookout. Maybe somewhere between the spray of tomato seeds and the pudding cleanup. What did it matter when? Point was, it had happened. Now, she had to contend with the complications.

She hadn't actually lied to Mike about her identity, but what she'd let him and everyone else, except Harold, assume could hardly be viewed as pure truth. But what choice did she have? The fact that something about her money struck a sour note with Mike didn't take a rocket scientist to figure out, and she certainly didn't need any more fame to go with her fortune.

Clearing up the misconception amounted to her

telling him the truth about her lottery windfall. The problems arising from that opened another kettle of worms.

Could she trust Mike with her secret? She barely knew him. And what she'd seen so far of his unpredictability didn't make her feel terribly secure with the idea of telling him who she was. For some strange reason, trusting him with her heart came a whole lot easier.

Why? That little inner voice every woman uses to guide her through life told her he'd never intentionally hurt her by divulging her secret. But Dave hadn't set out to tell the world her identity, either. And Harold, as discreet as he'd painted himself, had nearly spilled the beans at dinner. If she hadn't learned anything else in the past two months, she'd learned that good intentions paved the road to disaster.

Jackie sighed heavily and snuggled deeper into her blanket cocoon. Since the men had informed her the night before that they were all meeting friends at Tolley's for a pancake breakfast and another full day of football and food, she was in no hurry to crawl out of her warm bed.

However, as they had the night before—all night— her eyes popped open when thoughts of Mike intruded on her sleep. Sighing and stretching, she decided that if she hadn't solved the mystery last night, a few more hours of restless tossing and turning weren't going to change anything.

She climbed from the bed, slipped out of her flannel pajamas, then pulled on the sweats she'd bought during her trip to town with the men before the fish fry. Promising herself a shower right after her morning caffeine injection took hold, she shuffled toward the blanket opening.

Before she even drew back the flimsy partition, her nose caught the welcome aroma of fresh-brewed coffee. Coffee? All the men should have been gone. Next came the clatter of what sounded like typewriter keys.

Stepping into the great room, she spotted Harold immersed in his bookkeeping, his fingers flying over the keys of his ancient adding machine. She ambled toward him, rubbing her eyes.

"Good morning. I figured you'd be up soon," he mumbled, his eyes never leaving the figures on the tongue of white adding machine paper growing from the machine like some alien being. "Coffee's fresh. Help yourself."

"Thanks," she mumbled back, noting that his ears were turning a rosy pink. Would he ever get used to her?

Pouring herself a large mug of the revitalizing brew, she listened. The only sounds in the room came from the crackling logs in the fireplace and the metallic clatter of her spoon against the ceramic mug as she stirred her coffee. In an odd way, the silence comforted her.

She slipped into the chair opposite him. Luxuriating in the fireplace's warmth against her back, she sipped her coffee, studied Harold and allowed the caffeine to bring her tired body and mind to life.

Her mother had always said Jackie slept like the

dead and only an atom bomb could wake her. Today, it would have taken two atom bombs to erase the stupor of her sleepless night—or one Mike Hamilton, if the way he'd brought her to life in his arms yesterday meant anything. She neatly stuffed that thought safely out of thinking range. How on earth could anyone get that passionately inflamed with chocolate pudding running down her cleavage? Was she a pervert?

Thanks to Harold's strong brew, her body slowly came back to life. The renewed clatter of the adding machine broke into her disconcerting musings.

"Why aren't you at Tolley's with the others?"

He didn't look up. "My team lost."

"Sorry."

"What?" Glancing up, Harold's fingers stilled, then he waved away her sympathy with a flick of his hand. "I'm not really into football. I chose a team to…" He stopped dead and studied her for a long moment. "You look like…"

"Hell," she finished for him.

A familiar flush washed over Harold's cheeks. He nodded, pushed the machine aside, then pulled his mug in front of him. "That wouldn't have been my word choice, but…yes. You look like hell."

Jackie groaned. "Thanks. That's just what I needed to hear."

"Well, maybe this will help you feel more chipper." He sorted through some manila folders, then extracted one from the center of the pile. "I have that list of possible investments for you."

Jackie brightened, took another sip of coffee, then set the cup aside.

"As I see it, you need something that will utilize the bulk of your winnings."

"The bulk?" She become absorbed in the total transformation from shy to supremely confident that Harold went through each time they talked business.

"If you invest the bulk, it might just discourage the fortune hunters you say are harassing you."

She frowned.

"No ready cash for handouts."

Jackie brightened. She placed her palms on the table, pushed herself forward across the papers, then planted a loud kiss on Harold's forehead. "I love you, Harold. Will you marry me and be my devoted accountant?"

Sputtering, Harold shuffled the papers, then reshuffled them. His chubby cheeks flamed crimson and he chewed vigorously on his bottom lip. "I'm afraid I'm too set in my ways to consider marriage, even if you were serious." He finally looked at her. "But I do appreciate your enthusiasm."

Jackie patted his hand. "Well, I guess I'll have to settle for you just being my accountant." She squeezed his fingers. "And, my friend, thanks for keeping our little secret."

His pleased smile seemed to light up the room. "I'd be honored to be both."

"Okay. So now that you've turned me down and broken my heart, what exactly are these bulk investments you're talking about?"

Spreading out several sheets of paper, Harold explained to Jackie in detail the choices she had for putting her lottery winnings to use, and in doing so, remove the golden albatross hanging around her neck.

She scanned his list, then leaned back and sighed. "I'm a simple girl. I don't know anything about publishing houses and manufacturing firms."

"What about the hotel?"

She laughed. "Harold, you're looking at a girl who can't keep her own bedroom clean, much less a whole building full of them."

"Jackie."

She grinned inwardly. That was the first time he hadn't called her Ms. Barrett.

"There's a good deal more to running a hotel than the maid service."

"See? I told you I didn't know anything about it."

Jackie rose and replenished her coffee, then flopped back down in her chair. "I'm sorry. I know I'm being difficult, but there's just not a blasted thing on that list that sparks my interest."

Harold frowned and studied his list. "Here," he finally said, "here's just the thing. A chain of restaurants." He looked at her, his eyebrows arched expectantly.

She considered his suggestion for a moment, then shook her head. "Sorry. My passion is for cooking the food, not owning the restaurant that serves it."

"You could do both," he said hopefully.

"There's one problem with all the things on your list. They all have the potential for earning more money. Lots of money." She leaned on the edge of the table and stared down at him. "Hells bells, Harold, I can't handle what I have now. What am I gonna do with more?"

Restlessly, she paced, then took a seat on the fireplace's raised hearth and stared into the dancing flames. "Truth be known, my powers of concentration are shot today. I didn't get much sleep last night." She glanced at him. "Let me have the list. I'll look it over and then we can talk again in a few days."

Harold stuffed the papers resignedly back into the folder. He laid it on her side of the table. Pushing back his chair, he picked up his coffee mug, circled the table, then settled himself next to Jackie on the hearth.

"Heard there was a food fight in the kitchen last night." He made a tsk-tsk sound with his tongue. "Terrible waste of good food."

Jackie grabbed the poker. She jabbed at the glowing embers on a log. Sparks shot into the air, then drifted up the chimney with the smoke. The honeysweet odor of burning oak wafted out to her. She inhaled deeply, then poked again at the log, mesmerized by the shower of sparks that resulted from each prod. Sparks as hot as those she and Mike had generated. Her body warmed from a heat that had nothing to do with the burning logs.

"How long have you known Mike?"

Harold chuckled, as if her question didn't surprise him. "Four or five years."

"Did you know Ken before he died?" Jackie jabbed the logs again.

"Yes."

"What was he like?"

"The opposite of Mike. Ken liked to party, chase women, drink, take life on a day-to-day basis."

"And Mike?"

"Of the two, Mike took life more seriously. Responsible. Hard worker. He dated, but seldom. Went to parties sometimes with Ken, but didn't drink. He usually ended up driving Ken home." Harold had warmed to his subject. He grabbed her mug and his, refilled them, then came back to his seat on the hearth. "Ken enjoyed life. Mike never seemed to be able to let go long enough to enjoy it. That's why the food fight surprised me."

"Oh?" She glanced at the accountant's heat-infused face.

"It's something Ken would have done. Not Mike. Mike would have been the one to clean up the mess while Ken went off on his next adventure."

Jackie was silent. Her mind replayed the conversation she'd had with Mike about remodeling the kitchen.

"How did Ken die?" The question had haunted her for some time.

"Car accident. He'd been at a wedding reception with a rich tourist from one of the hotels. They'd both had too much to drink. She was driving and the car hit an icy patch of road. It skidded off an embankment. She came away with bruises and a few scratches. Ken died four hours later in the hospital.''

"One more thing he left unfinished," Jackie murmured.

"One more thing? I don't understand."

"His life. Unfinished." And Mike's trying to do it for him, she added silently, just as he always finished everything else for Ken. Suddenly, she understood much more about this complex man with whom she'd fallen in love.

MIKE PUSHED HIS WAY through a wall of pine boughs and stepped into the open meadow. He stopped short. A surge of pure delight forced a smile to his cold lips. On the ground in front of him lay Jackie, coated in snow from her head to her toes, her arms and legs spread wide, making snow angels.

She hadn't noticed him, so he luxuriated in watching her. Her hat had come off and snow clung to her hair and her face. On her cheeks, tiny beads of moisture sparkled in the early morning sunlight. Her designer jeans and red parka showed dark splotches where the snow had melted into the material. Disheveled, abandoned, self-indulgent...breathtaking.

The salon-pampered look was gone, taking with it her air of wealth. With her hair in disarray, her face glowing and free of makeup, she had an untamed aura about her, compounded by the innocence of a child. For a moment, he could fool himself into believing the barriers between them had magically disappeared, even though he knew differently.

Despite his warnings to himself, Mike's blood stirred. The tamped embers of the fire that had almost burned out of control the night before ignited. He wanted to join in her abandon play and forget the chores awaiting him. He wanted to feel as free as she looked.

"Is this a private party or can anyone join in?"

She started at the sound of his voice, but made no effort to excuse what she'd been caught doing. Instead, she rolled her eyes toward him and smiled. Excitement turned her irises a darker blue.

"Pull up a snowdrift and join the fun."

Mike lay down next to her. "I'm new at this, so I'm going to need some instructions."

Sitting up, Jackie stared down at him. "You never made snow angels when you were a kid?"

"No." He hadn't had time for games.

Jackie gazed down at him for a few more moments, then resumed her reclining position in the snow. "Spread your arms like so," she coached, arranging her arms at a right angle to her body. "Spread your legs. Now move your arms up and down and your legs back and forth."

Following her lead, he pendulumed his arms and legs. Snow seeped down the collar of his sheepskin jacket. The coolness felt good against his heated skin—heat that he wasn't sure came as a result of the exercise or Jackie's instructions to spread his legs.

"Okay. Now, we have to check out our masterpieces." Jackie sat up. "Be careful not to step in the indentations. You'll ruin the angel if you do." Care-

fully, she levered herself up, then reached out a hand
to him.

He grabbed it, then pushed himself to his feet. Together, they surveyed their handiwork.

"Botticelli couldn't have done better," she crowed.

"Who?"

"Botticelli. He was an Italian painter or sculptor or
something. Specialized, so I'm told, in Madonnas and
angels."

Mike had quit listening. The placement of the snow
angels held his attention. The two angels were joined.
He liked the idea of being joined to Jackie. He liked
it too damn much.

Jackie nudged him. She pointed at the wide skirt
on the taller of the two angels. "You look great in a
dress."

"And you, Ms. Barrett," he said with a grin that
matched hers, "have a smart mouth." Reaching
above her head, he grabbed a low, snow-laden pine
bough and shook it.

What snow didn't fall to her feet with a soft plop
went down the back of her neck.

"Why you..." She scooped up a handful of snow,
shaped it into a ball, then fired it at him, hitting him
square in the chest.

"Bad girl." Mike shook his finger and advanced
on her. "Now you have to be punished."

"Punished?"

"Bad girls get their faces washed with snow."

Squealing, Jackie ducked away from him. She took
off through the trees, dodging and running like an

NFL wide receiver headed for the goal line. Her high-pitched laughter rang out over the open meadow.

Hot on her heels, Mike's long legs ate up the distance between them. Hurtling through the air, he tackled her.

Their entwined bodies rolled over and over, snow coating them everywhere, like sugared doughnuts. They came to rest with Mike straddling her waist. He filled his hand with snow, then held it above her face.

"Take back the remark about the dress?"

Jackie giggled uncontrollably and shook her head. "Clothing makes the man," she choked out, holding her hands up to shield her face.

"Oh, I see. It's my masculinity that's in question here." He did his best imitation of the villain in a silent movie stroking his mustache. "Well, my dear, I'll just have to convince you otherwise," he cackled.

Convulsed with laughter, Jackie eyed him warily. The laughter died abruptly. "Convince me," she said softly.

Snow fell from his hand and landed on her mouth. She licked it away.

Mike sobered. He couldn't stop looking at her lips. Moist. Wet. Cold from the snow. She'd stopped laughing. Her warm gaze stole the breath from his lungs.

Snow clung to her lashes and brows. A wisp of wet hair curled against her forehead, making her appear the picture of innocence. But the flame in her eyes said otherwise. It shouted "bad girl," and there was no doubt in his mind that, if she wanted to, Jackie could be bad. So bad that she'd be good. Better than good.

She had a knack for making him feel like a kid just let out of school and, at the same time, a man confident of his strengths. Sometimes the resulting emotions threw him off guard, but not now. Not with her looking up at him as if he embodied every positive thing in the universe.

"Will you come with me?" he asked impulsively. "No questions asked?" He studied her face, expecting her to refuse. "Trust me." She smiled and nodded. "No questions."

"No questions."

Standing, he grabbed her hand, then pulled her to her feet. She slipped easily into his arms, as if she belonged there. Maybe she did. All he knew for sure was he didn't want this time with her to end and that if he didn't kiss her at this very minute, he'd regret it forever.

She smelled like fresh air and sunshine. Her lips were soft, cool and willing. Absorbing his heat, they warmed quickly under his. With no urging from him, her mouth opened like a baby bird's, eager, hungry. His body came alive with a need stronger than anything he'd ever experienced. Reluctantly, he raised his head.

Her eyes fluttered open. She gazed up at him with a dreaminess illuminating her eyes that nearly made him return to her soft mouth for more.

"Let's go," he murmured, before he lost all control.

NEARLY HALF AN HOUR LATER, Mike held back the lower limbs of a towering pine tree and urged Jackie into a small clearing. A tall sticklike structure dominated the center of the open space, reaching so far into the clear, cloudless sky that Jackie had to rock back on her heels to see the small building perched on top.

At the base of the structure, a sign had become almost completely covered by a snowdrift. Wiping away the snow, Jackie read it aloud. "Ranger Station 103, Department of Forestry."

"It's not used anymore," Mike said from her side. "When the state cut back its budget, this tower was one of many casualties of the reduced funds allocated to the Department of Forestry."

A note of sadness colored his tone, which, in turn, saddened her.

"If they closed the tower, how do they keep watch on the forest for fires and such?"

Mike pointed over her shoulder to a distant purple peak. His breath caressed the side of her face. "There's another tower over there."

A tension-fraught moment passed before she could marshal her senses and zero in on the mountain he pointed at. When his nearness became more than she could safely stand, she turned back to the tower.

For the first time, she noticed a set of footprints leading up to the bottom of the ladder built into the side of the tower's base, the only means of access to the building at the top.

"Looks like someone's been here recently."

"Those are mine." He grinned sheepishly. "I was here yesterday. I forgot the time, which accounts for why I didn't show up to help you." He took her hand, slipped off her mitten, then traced small circles on her palm with his thumb. "I really did intend to come back to help."

Sincerity glowed in the depths of his inky eyes. Jackie swallowed hard, then tore her gaze away from his. She glanced at the snow obliterating her feet and marveled that it hadn't melted. "Are we trespassing?"

"No." He led her to the bottom of the ladder. "When Ken bought Land's End, there was a clause that prohibited him from developing any more than five acres. This land is a part of the undeveloped section. When the Forestry Department deserted the tower, it became our property." He glanced up the ladder, then to Jackie. "Want to go up?"

Jackie eyed the ladder, thought about the total isolation waiting for them atop the tower, then glanced at Mike.

"You aren't afraid of heights, are you?" Mike asked.

The only thing tall that rattled her was Mike. "No. Heights don't bother me." *It's small, confining spaces shared with men who ooze sensuality that scare the bejesus out of me.*

"Up you go, then." He took her upper arm and steadied her while she stretched for the first rung of the ladder.

Why not go up? Her feet were about numb from

trudging through the snow. Frostbite held no appeal to her and definitely didn't qualify as a souvenir she wanted to take home. Heartbreak would cause enough pain.

She ascended the ladder, Mike close behind.

"Go slow. Your boots are snowy and the rungs are slick." He must have felt her muscles tighten under the hand he'd placed on her thigh to reassure her. "Don't be afraid. I'm right behind you."

Like I need him to verify that.

If he kept exhaling against the backs of her thighs and brushing the seat of her jeans with the top of his head...

"I'll catch you if you fall."

Too late. I'd already taken the tumble and the safety net was missing. When my heart kicked in and ignored my brain, two days ago, where were you hiding these protective instincts?

Her foot slipped. Mike's warm hands cupped her behind. The heat that flamed to her cheeks fanned out over every inch of her body. Neither her feet nor any other part of her was cold anymore.

"Concentrate on what you're doing," he chided from below. "This is no time to sightsee."

She glared down at his rakish grin. And exactly how did he expect her to concentrate on anything with his hand still gripping her buns?

Her expression must have spoken volumes about her dilemma. He moved his hand abruptly, then grabbed one of the rungs.

Slowly, she continued her climb, her mind struggling to stay centered on placing her feet and not the lingering effects of Mike's touch. When the sill of the fire-tower door loomed into her line of vision, she sighed with relief.

Mike followed her into the small interior. Awareness of him sprang back to life. There couldn't have been more than a few feet of empty floor space. If either of them tried to move about, they would be coming into more intimate contact than she could safely handle right now.

To take her mind off the situation, she glanced around her. The room was missing the smell of a building that had been left unoccupied for a long period of time. Rather, it held the fragrance of the open air. "How much time do you spend here?"

"Considerable," he admitted.

In the middle of the room stood a large, round, flat table. Big numbers ringed the outer perimeter. In the center an arrow-shaped pointer, closely resembling one hand of a clock, could be moved to coincide with any of the numbers. She assumed it helped pinpoint the location of forest fires.

In the far corner, a small kitchenette had been built in. The electric space-heater next to it would provide warmth for the duty ranger. A black, outdated telephone, its cord hanging unattached, resided on a bookcase with a flat worktop.

But the thing that her gaze kept skipping over was a small cot nestled in the corner where Mike stood watching her. She glanced hesitantly from the bare mattress to him.

"I didn't bring you here to ravage your body, if that's what your overactive little mind is thinking."

Why not?

She blinked. Did she just think that or had she blurted it out?

"Why *did* you bring me here?" she asked when she finally regained control of her powers of speech.

He walked to the window nearest him. "For this." Slowly, like a curtain rising on a stage, he raised the roll-up blinds. Little by little, as it crawled up the window, the breathtaking splendor of the mountains came into view.

One by one, Mike raised the shades on the windows. Each revealed more of the landscape. When he'd lifted the last one, nature surrounded them like an artist's mural. The Adirondack Mountains lay like a sleeping bride, decked out in snowy white, evergreens dotting her hair.

Born and raised in the Catskill Mountains of Upper New York State, Jackie wasn't immune to the beauty of nature. Not even their magnificence could surpass this visual feast. She glowed warmly with the knowledge that he'd chosen her to share it with—this private hideaway.

Moving closer to the window, she rested her palms on the chilly sill and scanned the horizon of purple snowcapped mountains.

"Lovely, isn't it?"

Mike's voice came from beside her ear. His warm breath, sweet with the lingering smell of spicy toothpaste caressed her cold skin. His hands, framing her hips, kept her from escaping either the view or him.

Her voice emerged husky, as if from a dream. "The night of the fish fry, you said you had nothing to give any woman." She placed her palms flat against the cold pane of glass. "You were so wrong. You have, Mike. You have all this."

His body stiffened against hers, then he moved away.

A chill invaded her clear to her bones, even though he'd turned on the heater at some point and the cold room had slowly warmed.

Chapter Eight

"There was a time when I would have agreed with you," Mike said, sitting on the cot at the far side of the fire-tower room.

He glanced at Jackie. She seemed totally captivated by the mountains. Her profile, outlined by the brilliant blue winter sky and the dazzling sunshine, was exquisite. The sun's rays turned her hair to burnished gold. He itched to touch it, to comb his fingers through the silky strands...while he kissed her senseless.

Instead, he ran frustrated fingers through his own overlong hair, then fisted his hand on his thigh. "I used to believe that the beauty beyond those windows was all a man needed to be happy."

"And now?"

"I grew up, got a taste of real life."

Jackie left the window. Her light footsteps drew near. His muscles tightened. She stopped a few feet in front of him.

"Why did you really bring me here?"

Hell, how was he supposed to answer her? Why

had he brought her here? He shook his head, then glanced at her. "I don't know. Maybe I wanted to share this with someone I thought would appreciate it."

"What about Ken?"

"What about him?"

"Didn't you share it with him?"

Her question threw him off balance. Sharing his dreams with Ken had never entered his mind. They'd always been too busy living Ken's to worry about Mike's. Would Ken have understood Mike's deep regard for the things around him? He doubted it. "Staring at the mountains doesn't make money. Selling reservations to tourists does."

She took another step. Tentative, as if wary of his reaction. "Tell me about Ken."

He stood, then moved to the other side of the cramped room. He needed space, beyond her aura, to think. Unfortunately, the tower wasn't designed to accommodate more than one person and the necessary equipment. "What about him? He was my brother."

"I know all that. Why did the two of you buy Land's End? Why not just Ken?"

Mike couldn't prevent the derisive laugh that broke from him. "Who knows? One day he decided he wanted a fishing camp. When we were discharged from the army, we pooled our savings and bought it." He stared out the window.

He wanted to buy the camp. A slip of the tongue or the naked truth coming to light? "Did *you* want the camp?"

"What the hell is this, the third degree?" Why was she asking all these questions? What difference did any of this make anymore? He answered her anyway.

"No."

"Then why?"

"There's no big mystery to this. Ken wanted it, so we bought it. End of story." He regretted the anger tinting his voice, but she was forcing him to look at things in a way in which he'd never seen them before, forcing him to answer questions left unanswered for too long.

"And what did Mike want?"

He glanced at her. Expecting to see... What was he expecting? Sympathy? Apathy? Whatever it was, neither of those things showed on her face. Instead, genuine interest was reflected in her expression. It had been years since anyone cared what he wanted, or thought—or dreamed.

"I was going to enter the Forestry Service. I wanted to take care of all this." His hand swept the vista beyond the windows.

"So why didn't you?"

He continued to stare out the window. Why? Because Ken would never have lasted on his own. "I just didn't. That's all." His sudden surge of anger surprised him. Not anger at Jackie, but anger at his brother. Anger at the man who had saddled him with a secondhand dream, then died.

But had Ken saddled Mike with his dream or had he just allowed his brother to do so? The room suddenly became too hot. He shrugged out of his jacket, then threw it on the cot. Turning back to the window, he looked into a past he didn't really want to see.

"Mike." Her hand lay on his arm. He jumped. He hadn't even heard her approach. She, too, had shed her parka. "Why didn't you ever make snow angels?"

Such an innocent question and so many complicated answers. Should he tell her that you need time to be a child, to play a child's games? That he'd never gotten that chance? That his father had run out on his family when Mike was thirteen, forcing Mike into the role of father and brother, watching over Ken while his mother worked. That when Ken got a job at the corner grocery store to buy a bike, then quit when he had the bike, Mike had taken Ken's place. And then, when he lost interest in the bike, Mike had used it as his transportation back and forth to a job he never wanted, but felt compelled to assume for Ken.

Was that what she wanted to hear? He wanted to tell her. He wanted to tell someone. But he'd kept it buried inside himself for too long and breaking old habits didn't come easy.

"I guess I considered it girl stuff."

Evasion. Jackie dropped her hand from his sleeve. He'd wanted to talk. She knew he had. She'd spend every cent she had to find out what had been tripping through his mind in those few quiet moments.

For a long time, neither of them spoke. They stared off into the distance. Beyond them lay a beauty that, if not safeguarded by someone like Mike, could never be replaced. Once destroyed, it would be lost forever to future generations—children who would never see clear winter skies unobscured by exhaust fumes from too many cars; evergreens that didn't smell like plastic and reside in department-store windows; animals roaming wild and unfettered by iron bars; or fish swimming in clear, unpolluted streams.

Sadness for this man whose only dream had been to protect that legacy overcame Jackie.

Below them, a gray fox entered the clearing, sniffed at their footprints, glanced at the tower, then, apparently losing the scent of his quarry, disappeared into the thick forest.

Like the fox, Mike had surrendered his goal, but not for lack of direction. He'd given it up out of misplaced loyalty to a brother he loved, a brother who didn't appreciate the sacrifice.

Jackie finally figured out what it was that Mike needed. Mike needed a new dream, a dream of his own.

As she stared after the fox, her mind churned with ideas and slowly one began to take shape. Preposterous? Maybe. Do-able? She wouldn't know that until she talked to Harold. As the idea grew and gained substance, she knew in her heart that it could well represent the answer to her problems and, if he co-operated, Mike's, as well.

A bubble of happiness welled up inside her, expanding at an alarming rate. She began to understand the sheer delight of doing something important for someone you love. Perhaps that's why Dave had tried so hard to care for her, in his own bumbling way.

Perhaps that's why Mike had sacrificed all for his brother.

Along with the excitement of her plan came a new feeling of freedom, the likes of which she hadn't experienced, even before the lottery win. Impulsively, she turned to share it with Mike. Before the words could pass her lips, the look on his face killed them.

As he surveyed the landscape laid out before him a love reflected in his features, a love the depth of which she had never witnessed before. Envy bit down on her happiness. Would he ever look at her like that? Like he'd move heaven and earth to be a part of her? To nurture her? To protect her? To cherish her? To love her?

Mike could feel Jackie's gaze on him, but he couldn't meet it. In the past few minutes, he'd come to a startling realization, one that shook him worse than the bank turning down his bid for the second mortgage on Land's End.

He loved Jackie Barrett.

He loved the most unlikely, most inappropriate, most unreachable, most understanding, most empathetic woman of his acquaintance.

It had coiled in his gut the moment he'd first seen her sitting on that bed, legs crossed like a little girl at play. It had tugged at his heart that night with Shag and again this morning while they rolled in the snow. He'd felt it over and over, but then, as now, he'd told his heart the futile emotion could lead nowhere.

He had nothing to give Jackie except a used-up, forgotten dream, a run-down fishing camp and a quiet, uneventful life in the wilderness of the Adirondacks. A city girl like Jackie would shrivel and die in this isolation like a hothouse flower in a snowbank.

But the more he remained near her, the more the light fragrance of her perfume curled around him, the more he gazed into her lovely face, the more he wanted to believe he was wrong. He wanted to accept that they could have a future, a tomorrow.

Slowly, he pivoted to face her. His heart thudded heavily inside his chest. Apprehension? Anticipation?

Jackie stared silently back at him from a face haloed in sun-kissed curls. Gold-tipped lashes framed her sky-blue eyes, eyes misty with emotion and darkening with a plea that matched the one rising in him. Her cheeks still held the flushed evidence of the cold wind and their romp in the snow. Her lips, lacking the artificial coloring of lipstick, glistened cherry red, as if she'd just moistened them.

Acting on an impulse too strong to deny, he framed her face with his hands and drew her mouth to his. Before their lips met, he made a promise to himself. *Just a kiss. Just for today. Just for this moment.*

She accepted his kiss eagerly, as if she had been as hungry for it as he. Her fingers burrowed into his hair. With the tip of his tongue, he begged admittance into the honey-sweet warmth he remembered. Easily, her mouth opened to his gentle request.

Releasing her face, he slid his arms around her, gathering her into the heat of his body. She fit. They fit, like two precision-crafted pieces of a jigsaw puzzle.

He moved his hands over her back. So small. So fragile. So... He feared hurting her, but she tightened her arms around his neck and pulled him closer. Her small breasts burned through the fabric of his wool shirt and into his flesh. Her thighs scorched his jeans-clad legs.

He told himself to stop while he could, while he still had the strength to push her away, while he still had the sense to let go of the best thing that had ever touched his life. But he couldn't. He raised his head for much-needed air.

"Mike?"

His name slid off her tongue as a whispered plea.

"What?"

"You were kissing me."

"You noticed."

"You lied."

He gazed down into her lovely face. "No, I underestimated how totally sexy one small woman could be and how stupid I've been for denying us something we've both wanted."

She smiled. Not just with her mouth, but with her entire face, as though he'd just bestowed some precious gift on her. Any control he might have held in reserve beat a hasty retreat. A husky growl rumbled from deep within his chest.

"No one has ever said anything like that to me before." She outlined his bottom lip with the tip of a manicured nail. The soles of his feet tingled with the effect.

Opening his mouth, he nipped at her fingertip, then

sucked it between his lips. She tasted salty-sweet. Keeping her gaze locked on his, she slowly withdrew her finger. Mike shuddered.

She frowned. "Would you mind terribly if I wasn't as proficient in bed as you accused me of being that first day?" She lowered her gaze to his chest. "That is if we're going to...if you want to... You know what I mean."

Mike laughed outright, then hugged her close. "You have to admit, you asked for that." He kissed the tip of her nose. "And, no, I don't mind a bit."

Secretly, her naivety fed his masculinity and roused his protective instincts.

Suddenly, the implications of her question hit him like a lightning bolt. He raised his head and pulled back to stare down at her.

"Is my imagination going haywire or did you just hint that there's some chance we might make love?"

She giggled softly. He loved the sound of her laughter. It trickled over him, renewing him like a fresh spring rain. She buried her face in his shoulder.

Jackie wasn't at all good at this sort of thing. The few sexual encounters she'd had at college had been orchestrated by overeager young men, who had barely removed their clothing, leaving her to conclude that sex was a highly overrated activity.

But not with Mike. She soared with Mike, like a bird turned loose to explore the limitless skies. Mike made her heart race, her body ache, her blood sing through her veins. Mike made her want to give, as well as receive.

"Well, is that what you were implying?" His lips moved against the top of her head.

She snuggled closer, hoping to convey with her body what she prayed he wouldn't ask her to put into words. She wanted Mike—craved him. When the ridge of his arousal nudged her belly, the fire that had been smoldering in her lower extremities suddenly flared into full flame, burning away her inhibitions.

"There's nothing wrong with your imagination." That was the best she could do without blatantly begging him to carry her to the cot and make love to her for the rest of the afternoon.

He stepped back, his hands gripping her hips. The smoldering desire mirrored in his velvet eyes made her tremble with anticipation. He wanted her, too.

Wordlessly, as if reading her mind, he scooped her into his arms, then carried her to the cot. Carefully, he set her down on the small bed.

"If I'm presuming too much, tell me now."

She smiled again and held out her hand in invitation. "The only thing you are is too slow."

Still he hesitated. "I can't promise you anything beyond today," he said, his voice raspy with the effort of holding back.

"I know," she whispered, her heart aching.

Today she'd know the ecstasy; tomorrow she'd learn to live with the pain.

When he still made no move to join her, she levered herself to her knees in front of him, then took the top button of his shirt between her fingers. She pushed it through the first buttonhole. Then followed suit with the next button, and the next. Inch by tantalizing inch, his chest bared before her hungry gaze.

Jackie skimmed her knuckles across the matt of black hair forming a perfect triangle in the middle of his chest. Her hand went lower. His stomach muscles contracted. She smiled up at him, reveling in this small taste of feminine power.

Testing his reaction, she slowly slipped his shirttails from the waistband of his jeans. When it drifted soundlessly to the floor, they ignored it. She flattened her palms on his chest, then slid them up to his collarbone, savoring the feel of taut muscle that lay just beneath the surface of his skin. Then she ran her hands over his shoulders and down his arms. Her small hands didn't come close to spanning his rockhard biceps. The strength she felt there sent a shiver of awareness through her.

Mike cupped her chin and raised her gaze to his. Bending, he kissed her mouth, softly. "I'd never hurt you," he murmured, misreading her trembling.

He kissed her again. As his mouth explored hers with an insatiable hunger, he caught the hem of her sweater in his fingers. Very slowly, relinquishing her lips for just a moment, he pulled the garment up and off. She heard the whisper of its flight to the floor to rest beside his shirt.

Jackie expected embarrassment. Even in college, she'd never been completely naked with a man. The few guys she'd dated never seemed to have time for foreplay. But with Mike, the embarrassment never came, not even when he looked down at the gentle swell of her breasts above the bra's lace-edged cups.

She held her breath and waited for him to touch her there. God, she needed him to touch her, to feel that fire shoot through her blood, as she knew it would.

When he finally bent and kissed her flesh, the sensations that streaked through her were nothing like those she'd imagined. Where the tingling and beginning of awareness had been, a full-fledged inferno of blazing desire took its place and raged throughout her. Shamelessly, she buried her hands in his hair and pulled his mouth closer to her.

The ache started in her throat, fanned out into her chest, then arrowed downward to the V of her thighs. Her back arched and a tiny animal-like sound escaped her lips. Mike swamped her senses, turning her into a mindless wanton.

He laved the soft flesh, feeling and hearing the brush of lace against his beard stubble. He savored the lingering traces of perfume in her cleavage, and when an image of her applying it flittered through his mind, he smiled against her skin.

Soft. Warm. Intoxicating. Not enough words. Not enough ways to describe this incredibly sensuous woman. She raced through his blood like a drug, bringing him to life as he'd never known life before. Coloring his gray world, then standing it on its end.

Greedily, he suckled her skin. He needed more, so much more. He needed to be inside her. To feel her warmth singeing him, cradling him, gloving him.

He slid his hands beneath her to unclasp her bra. Her back arched like an angry little kitten. When he peeled away the fabric, a fervent moan issued from her.

Gazing down at her naked breasts, each crowned by a perfect, tawny, pebble-hard nipple, he wondered what it would be like to have Jackie's warmth in his bed every night to chase away the tensions of the day. He glanced at her face. She stared at him, eyes sleepy with desire. The throb in his groin increased.

"Touch me."

Her whispered plea, nearly inaudible, could have been drowned out by the slightest sound. But he heard it. He heard it and complied.

Gathering her in his arms, he lifted her from the bed and held her against him. Where their skin touched, fire radiated in scorching fingers of energy. The soft mounds of her breasts seared him.

She threw her head back, eyes closed, an open invitation for him to do as he pleased. Eagerly, he bowed his head and rained soft, nibbling kisses over her neck, her collarbone, her upper chest. Eventually, his mouth found the hardened peak of one breast and captured it between his lips.

Jackie squirmed and moaned. Mike alternated his attention from one breast to the other. Lowering her to the mattress, he closed his hand around her other breast, massaging and stroking.

"Mike, please. I hurt."

He hurt, too. His entire body ached with the need

to go farther. At the same time, he didn't want this magic to end.

But this wasn't the kind of pain that could be cured with a few aspirin. This ache went deeper, right to his very soul. He wanted Jackie, but not just for an afternoon. He wanted her forever. But since that wasn't an option, he'd gladly settle for a few hours that would be seared in his memory, as if with a branding iron, for all eternity. For one afternoon, he'd love Jackie. For one afternoon she'd be his.

Levering himself off the edge of the bed, he stood and unclasped the waistband of his jeans. She watched through smoldering, slitted eyes. Impatiently, he shed his clothes, then stood naked before her.

His arousal told her without words the effect she had on him. Lord, but he was beautiful. His muscles flowed and quivered with the same fluid motion Shag's had. He held himself proudly, just like the stag did, and around the edges lingered a hint of the same wildness.

Her fingers went to the fastening of her own jeans, but he pushed her hands away. "That's my job. I want to watch as your skin appears an inch at a time and savor every moment."

When his fingers slid across the sensitive flesh of her belly, she sucked in her breath and closed her eyes. Seeing only with her mind intensified the sensations his touch aroused in her. Her boots slid off her, as if in a dream. Next came her jeans and socks. Then her panties. Slowly, ever so slowly, he guided the wisp of silk down her body, then off her feet.

His fingers caressed her knees, then moved up to her thighs, then higher still to the warm dampness, proof positive of her need.

And then, he was there, his naked body next to hers, heating her to a degree far beyond measuring, far beyond imagining. His palm covered her. His fingers tested her wetness. She wanted to cry out for him to end this torture, but his mouth had descended on hers and his tongue stroked her in time to the movement of his probing fingers.

She circled his back with her arms. Tension built in her belly and radiated out over her entire body. Her fingers dug deep into his flesh. Her mind filled with the need for release.

Then, like a shower of sparks, she was bathed in sensations so strong that they stole her breath, her thoughts, her will.

Mike held tight to Jackie as the first waves of her climax overcame her. When she stilled, he eased himself above her, position himself at her opening and then entered the haven of her body.

For a moment, he lay motionless, unable to move, unable to cope with the sensations rocketing through him. God, he'd known it would be good, but nothing like this. Nothing like this eternity of mindless wonder, this overwhelming feeling of forever.

Slowly, he began to move. Jackie arched toward him, her fingers gripped his arms, digging into his skin. He felt nothing but the hot, wet caress of her around him.

Time disappeared, taking with it Land's End, re-

sponsibility and the sameness of the day-after-day repairs. A growing hum filled his head. Then, like a
giant skyrocket, sensation exploded in a shower of
lights.

As tremor after tremor of release shook her body,
Jackie cried out his name and clung to him. And when
the storm had abated and they lay spent and exhausted, they still held on tight, each knowing that
the afternoon had ended, and that tomorrow would
mark the beginning of an empty eternity of lonely
hours.

Chapter Nine

On the way back from the fire tower Jackie and Mike talked—about trees, mountains, birds, animals and wildflowers—but not a word was said about them or what had just occurred. Although it bothered Jackie that Mike studiously avoided the subject of their love-making, she had to admit that the topic of their afternoon together was not something she was ready to delve into, either. Still a small part of her hated that neither of them felt comfortable with what had happened.

At the main lodge, Mike kissed her tenderly and mumbled, "See ya," then strode off in the direction of the woodpile that fed the many fireplaces at Land's End. His kiss tasted like goodbye. With a sinking heart, she could physically sense the barrier—the wall Mike used to protect himself—go up between them. Had she been wrong about how he felt? Did he regret confiding in her about Ken? But most of all, did he regret making love to her? His actions seemed to say that he did.

A few moments later, the resonating sound of an

ax forcefully splitting logs insinuated itself into the wintry stillness.

Jackie stared mutinously in the direction of the noise. She'd be damned if she'd humiliate herself further by chasing down a man who was so pigheaded that he couldn't see a good thing when it jumped up and bit him. "I will not go after him. I will not!"

Seconds after the avowal passed her trembling lips, she had covered most of the frozen ground between herself and the old stump where Mike split wood.

"That's it? See ya? That's all you have to say after we...after.... Well, you know." Why couldn't she say it? Made love. And no matter what Mike Hamilton said, they had *not* just had sex. *They'd made love, damn it.*

Mike looked up from balancing a log atop the stump. His face looked strained. His dark eyes had lost their luster. He'd shed his jacket and carelessly rolled his sleeves past his elbows in fat, uneven folds. As he hefted the ax above his head, the muscles in his forearms throbbed with the weight. A frown creased his wide forehead. His lips thinned.

"Let it go, Jackie."

He swung the ax down hard. The wood split like a ripe melon and fell to the snowy earth, mimicking Jackie's heart as it broke apart inside her chest.

"Let it go?" Unable to do as he commanded, she paced the hard ground, trying to control her frustration. Throwing him a puzzled frown, she paused, then placed mittened hands on her hips and faced him squarely. "Tell me, exactly how do I do that? How do I casually dismiss two of the most..." She stopped short of telling him how much those hours had meant to her. No matter what, she couldn't do that, couldn't expose herself so completely. "How do you forget two hours of your life?"

"Don't ask questions you don't want to hear the answers to."

The advice her father had given her over and over triggered warning bells in her mind. She ignored it and plunged on.

"How do you do it, Mike? Was that just a quick roll in the hay for you? Something to ease your libido? Something to—"

Before she could finish, Mike had dropped the ax, crossed the few feet of ground that separated them, then took her upper arms in his strong hands. He glared down at her with his burning ebony gaze. His jaw muscles worked spasmodically, as if he fought to control himself in some way. Ironically, as angry as his face painted him, his grip was gentle.

"Don't ever say that again...ever."

Jackie's heart did a hopscotch beat. She swallowed hard. Her throat hurt with the tangled emotions fighting to rise. "Then tell me what it was."

Mike let her go abruptly. He turned back to the wood waiting to feel the bite of his ax, but his interest in burning off the emotions plaguing him had vanished.

How he wanted to tell her that those hours with her had already been consigned to a part of his memory where, when life began to close in, he could pull them out and savor the comfort they'd bring. He wanted to tell her that never in his life had he experienced such joy, such contentment, such freedom as he had in her arms.

But he couldn't. Telling her would only feed the hope shining in her eyes. And there was no hope.

"It was a...mistake."

Her gasp—surprise? disbelief? outrage?—cut through him as surely as if he'd turned the ax on himself.

"Why?"

He'd decided days ago that if there was a question to be asked about anything, Jackie would ask it. Normally, her inquisitive mind delighted him—but not now. Not now when the answers would tear them both apart, emotionally and physically.

"Because we can't give each other anything but heartache."

Silence enfolded them.

"You're wrong." Her voice came to him as if born on a soft spring breeze from far away.

"I wish I were."

"You don't know how wrong you are."

Silence again. Nothing but their breathing. Nothing but the lonesome sound of the wind high in the pines.

"*I* can give more. *I* can give you my love."

Joy exploded inside Mike like a Fourth of July rocket. Had he heard the words or only imagined them because he wanted to hear them?

The joy faded to despair. Either way, it didn't matter. Jackie had her life and he had his—sorry as it was—and they traveled down different roads that ran in opposite directions. He had to make her see that.

He pivoted toward her. She was gone. Maybe he had just dreamed the words, after all. Nevertheless, he tucked them away with the memories of an afternoon with the only woman he would ever love.

JACKIE RAN BLINDLY from Mike's rejection and her own admission. She pushed her hair from her eyes. The lingering scent of Mike's cologne still clung to her skin. An unbearable ache welled up inside her, then spread throughout her body. How would she stand this utter loneliness? Why had she been foolish enough to expect Mike to return her love?

A sudden longing for contact with the familiar, with one of the three people she could always count on to love her unconditionally, overwhelmed her. Turning back toward the lodge, she hurried up the front stairs, swung open the massive pine door, then stepped into the front foyer.

Heading straight for the reception desk, she slipped her gloves off, then crammed them in her pocket. Picking up the receiver of the old black phone, she dialed a number from memory. While the ringing phone sounded in her ear, she glanced around.

The lodge was old, perhaps going back three-quarters of a century, but solid. Massive pine beams spanned the low ceiling. In spots, bleached areas spoke of where the mounted heads of animals had once covered the walls. Knowing Mike and his love of nature, she surmised he'd removed them.

The mullioned windows lacked draperies or curtains, and the naked panes made the room look cold and inhospitable. Wide plank, pine floors badly needed a coat of wax. Scatter rugs, some flat, some bunched, as if someone had walked over them, dislodged them, then went on without straightening them, showed distinct signs of time and use. Dust covered everything, a silent message of abandonment. The room smelled...neglected.

The phone rang several times before she heard the decisive click signaling someone had picked up on the other end.

"D.J.'s. Dave speaking."

Her brother's cheery voice sluiced over her like a hot shower, warming the chilled corners of her heart.

"Hey, big brother. What's doin'?" Even to her own ears, the lightness she tried to inject into her voice sounded forced.

"Jack-in-the-box! How are you?"

His childhood nickname for her told Jackie without him saying so that he, too, felt the ache of their separation.

"Fine. I just wanted to check in and see if Marty's chased away all of my faithful following." Keeping the tremble from her voice was a near impossibility, but she fought to hold it to a minimum.

"Hey! Don't be picking on Marty. He's one of the best chefs around. I was lucky to snag him to help out while you're off in the mountains playing snow bunny.''

She shifted her weight and leaned her elbows on the dusty desk. "Being a snow bunny is hard work. It's not easy looking beautiful twenty-four hours a day, you know."

Dave laughed, as she knew he would. His sense of humor helped get her past his bumbling personality, then find forgiveness for the stupid things he did. Thank goodness his ineptitude in other areas didn't extend to his astute business sense.

"So, how do you like your cabinmates?"

"Ah, I wanted to talk to you about them. They're all wonderful, but you didn't tell me you were sending me off to play Snow White of the Adirondacks."

He chuckled. "It was one of those details you were better off not knowing."

Another of those details being the tall, darkly rugged camp owner? she wanted to ask. Instead, she evaded the issue entirely. "I suppose."

"Do I hear a *but* hanging on the end of that?"

Jackie smiled. Dave could always sense when she wasn't being totally truthful.

"Buts? No. No buts." The background noise of the busy restaurant made her check her watch. Supper hour. Dave's busiest time of day. "Well, I'd better let you go. I can hear that you're doing a booming business, so Marty must be doing something right."

Her pitiful joke didn't dissuade him. "Wait! Don't hang up." The background noise faded. He must have take the phone into the cloak room, something he often did to talk in private. "What's the problem, Jack?"

Sometimes Dave's innate ability to read his sibling could be a liability. This was one of those times. "I told you, I just wanted to check in. I had the insane idea that you might be wondering if I'd been eaten by a bear or carried off by a mountain lion."

"Jack, never kid a kidder. It goes without saying that I miss you, little sister. And you know Marty's capabilities. You recommended I hire him to fill in for you. Want to try again?"

Jackie covered her face with her free hand. How do you tell your big brother that you spent the afternoon making love with a man who suddenly can't put enough distance between you?

"Homesick, I guess?"

"Nope. No sale."

Silence. Nothing came to mind that her brother wouldn't see through in a minute. Before she could manufacture another excuse, Dave took a guess on his own—with unerring accuracy. "Do I sense man problems here, sister dear?" Jackie stalled for time. "Damn it, Jack, answer me. I can hear your heart breaking all the way down here."

Jackie tried to answer, but the huge lump in her throat blocked speech. She glanced around the foyer, as if an answer resided somewhere in its dark, dusty corners. Not until she looked back at the phone did she realize everything had blurred behind the moisture in her eyes.

Damn Mike Hamilton! What has he done to me? I never cry. Never!

As if her life didn't look bleak enough, now her mascara would run and she'd resemble a woebegone raccoon. She swiped angrily at her eyes with the cuff of her jacket sleeve, sniffed loudly, then glared at the black smear on the red material.

"It's not Tony, is it?" Dave's voice had risen in volume. "Did he make a pass at you?"

She could envision Dave as clearly as if he stood beside her. He'd assumed his protective-brother stance—back stiff as a board, shoulders squared, chin out, the gleam of inflicting bodily injury on someone in his Barrett-blue eyes.

"No. Doc keeps a short rein on Tony's male hormones."

Dave sighed audibly. "Okay, so Tony's out of the running. Then who?"

Obviously, he wasn't about to give up. One thing Jackie knew about Dave, when he dug in his heels, all hell couldn't budge him. She had no choice, other than just hanging up on him. "It's Mike."

Dead silence filled the phone.

"Mike Hamilton?"

"The same."

"Jeez, Jack."

"It's okay, big brother. He's not interested in your little sister."

"But my little sister is interested in him."

A short pause followed his question. *Interested* hardly covered the way she felt about Mike. "Yes."

"But he isn't. Are you sure he doesn't feel the same way?"

Am I sure? Only about as sure as I am that the sun will come up tomorrow morning.

"Believe me, he's not interested. He's got some hang-up about rich women because of his brother Ken's accident."

"Does he know? About the lottery, I mean?"

"No."

"Well, for Christmas sakes, Jack, tell him. You aren't anything like that dame. I know. I was at that reception. I met her."

She sighed. "That's not the problem. It's the damn money." She picked absently at a stamp on a letter addressed to Mike from the local bank.

"Jackie, I wish I could turn the time back to the day I talked you into buying that lottery ticket with the dollar you found." His voice thickened with emotion. "I'm sorry as hell, kid. But I can't, and you can't run from the winnings, either, so we'll both have to live with the consequences." He chuckled, the mirth conspicuously absent from the sound. "Do you remember how we used to wish we could live like the rich and famous? Now, at least you can. And all either of us can do is bitch."

Jackie sniffed again. "Pitiful, isn't it?" She half smiled. "If only Mike knew just how poor I was before I won that lottery."

"Tell him."

She straightened, placed the envelope back on the pile of unopened mail, stared at the phone as if it had taken on human qualities, then pressed it back to her ear. "What?"

"I said, tell him. If you tell Mike, he'll have to see that you're just a middle-class working woman."

"I'm not sure that'll make any difference. Besides I don't know him that well."

You knew him well enough to make love with him.

She ignored the nagging logic of the voice inside her head. "How can I be sure he won't say anything to anyone else and have this leak its way back to the press? I'm just not up to that again. Not to mention that I want Mike to accept me for me, whether that's Jacqueline Barrett, millionairess, or Jackie Barrett, middle-class gourmet chef."

She could almost hear Dave impatiently raking his fingers through his blond curls. "Jackie, you've never run from anything you could beat. It's one of the things I've always admired about you. You can beat this stereotypical image Mike has of rich women. I know you can. Prove to him that Jackie Barrett is a prize worth winning." He paused. "If this matters that much to you, you don't have a choice. You have to take a chance."

MIKE WAITED beside the corner of the lodge until Jackie faded into the trees bordering the guest parking lot. It hurt to look at her and not be able to go after her, sweep her into his arms, carry her off to the tower, then make love to her until the ache inside him went away.

Mike shoved his hands in his pockets and cast a

quick glance in her direction. They were both better off this way. She'd go back to her fancy life in the city in a couple of weeks and, after a few cocktail parties with her friends, she'd forget she ever knew a rough-hewn woodsman like him. And he'd be so busy that he wouldn't have time to think about a magical afternoon in a fire tower, to miss her, to regret letting her go.

Right! And tomorrow morning you'll wake up and Land's End will be Buckingham Palace.

The pain growing in his chest increased. Not a physical pain. It went deeper, right to his soul. He'd pushed away the woman he loved. He'd had to.

What could he offer Jackie? Another man's dream? A life of isolation and a few stolen hours in a fire tower? Women needed more. They needed security, a home they could be proud to show off to friends and neighbors; they needed kids, a future. Hell, he wasn't sure he had a future. He wasn't even sure Mike Hamilton existed anymore, or had ever existed, for that matter.

THAT EVENING, Mike slumped in a leather chair in the lounge, staring fixedly into the flames of a blazing fire. He sipped absently at the beer bottle clutched in his fingers. The cold bitter brew hadn't helped his sour mood, nor had it washed away the images of Jackie.

The door burst open, letting in a gust of frigid air and Peppy, his normal, starched posture bent to ward off the cold.

"Starting to drizzle," he announced.

Mike grunted in reply. He really didn't want company.

"With these temperatures, it'll turn to ice in no time."

Mike grunted again.

"Quite the conversationalist," Peppy chided, reverting to his usual gruff manner.

"Nothing in the rules of Land's End says that the owner has to be congenial."

Mike's gaze never left the fire. Strange, with his stocking feet perched on the hearth and thermal underwear beneath his jeans and wool shirt, he couldn't seem to rid himself of the chill that had seeped into his body, a chill that went right to his bones.

Grabbing a log from the pile in the basket next to him, Mike tossed the wood onto the fire. Flames shot up and engulfed the dry wood. The odor of pine drifted out to him. Firelight danced over the walls and the darkened room, producing eerie shadows that matched his mood.

Peppy took a seat in the chair opposite him, undaunted by his host's less than amiable greeting. "Wanna talk about it?"

Surprised by Peppy's offer, Mike glanced at him. The retired colonel never impressed him as the type to encourage confidentialities. Now, he seemed eager to talk. Problem was, Mike wasn't. "Not particularly."

"Hell, somebody best start getting this off their

chest. Jackie's sitting down at the cabin looking like she just lost the battle of the century.''

Mike ears perked. Jackie was brooding? He hated that she was unhappy. Hated it, but hadn't the power to change it. He took a swig of the beer, then let his arm drop lifelessly over the side of the overstuffed chair.

"And you look like you got caught in the cross-fire."

Not far off. Despite his grim thoughts, Mike had to smile at Peppy's putting a military spin on things.

Peppy leaned forward, rested his elbows on his knees, then clasped his hands together between them. He, too, stared into the leaping flames.

"Since you're not in the mood to talk, maybe you'll listen." His out-of-character mellow tone captured Mike's attention as the old colonel's bluster never had. "I spent two years of my life scared spit-less."

Mike's mouth fell open. He frowned at his fireside companion. Scared? The irascible Peppy? It occurred to him that Peppy might be winding up to spin one of his endless war stories. Mike wasn't in the mood to listen. "Occupational hazard," he murmured, hoping to discourage the tale to come.

With a swipe of his hand, Peppy waved away Mike's response. "Not scared of fighting or guns or even dying. Hell, I grew up in a family of men who were born with a rifle attached to their shoulders. Had my first .22 when I was five. Killed a rat three days later."

He leaned back in the chair and crossed his ankle over his knee. "I was scared of Martha."

"Martha? Your wife?"

Peppy nodded solemnly. "One and the same."

Mike had never met Martha, but he'd talked to her on the phone. To him, she'd always sounded like everyone's grandmother.

"From the first time I laid eyes on her, she scared the spit right out of me."

That a mere woman could scare Peppy had Mike doubting the authenticity of the story. "Scared? You? By a woman?"

Peppy nodded sagely. "You see, from the first time I looked at her, I knew she had the power to turn my life upside down and shake the stuffing out of it." He pointed a finger at Mike. "'Pears to me like that little lady down there has you running just as scared as I was."

Opening his mouth to deny Peppy's claim, Mike snapped it closed. It takes a skunk to smell a skunk. That the men had invested a lot of time encouraging a relationship between him and Jackie had not entirely escaped Mike's notice. Peppy was obviously their envoy. Rather than fight it, Mike resigned himself to listening.

"I don't need to be a detective to see that you two have spent the better part of the last few days twisting each other into knots."

"Yeah. Well, we started something that turned out would have been better off left alone. I don't have time for complications like that right now." He took another long drink of his beer, then set the empty bottle on the floor beside the chair.

"There's always time for love, my boy." Peppy touched Mike's arm. "Ken's gone, Mike. It's time you started living your life for *you*. If this place is dragging you down, sell it. Find yourself a job that doesn't drain your life's blood from your veins." He let go and stood. "Don't let that little lady get away."

Mike raised his gaze to him.

"Something in here," he said, jabbing his chest, "tells me she's special. Special doesn't come along very often. You need to reach out and grab it before it disappears."

As Peppy started toward the door, Mike stopped him. "How did you do it?"

Peppy laughed. "I didn't. I courted Martha for two years, scared as a rabbit the whole time. Martha got tired of waiting for me to pop the question, so she cornered me in my old '47 Oldsmobile one night and ask me to marry her. Said she wouldn't get out till I agreed. It was ten forty-five. Her father would have shot me where I stood if Martha stayed out past eleven o'clock." He laughed again, a deep, happy sound. "And she darn well knew it. I always figured she timed it that way."

Peppy being brought to task by a woman brought a curve to Mike's lips.

"That little termagant can still back me into a corner and bring me to attention, but I haven't regretted for one minute choosing her as my lifemate."

"Then why do you leave her every year and come up here for a month?"

"Hell, boy, even a kid needs a break from a candy store once in a while. All that sweetness can get to a man." He started to open the door, then changed his mind.

"Truth be known, Martha insists I take this furlough. She says I tend to get so caught up in the business of living that I forget to live. Says this time away from her and the girls makes me appreciate them more." He chuckled deep in his throat. "I hate to admit it, but she's right. Every now and again, you gotta do a little housekeeping, sort through things. Keep what's important, get rid of the clutter."

The door closed softly behind Peppy. Mike turned back to his contemplation of the flames. Peppy's parting words reverberated through Mike's mind. He threw another log on the fire, then looked around.

How much of this was clutter?

Chapter Ten

Rip and Adam stood back, arms crossed over their chests, deep thought furrowing their brows. Rip leaned a hip against a loose two-by-four propped against the stern of the boat. The craft shifted precariously in its cradle as he grabbed the doorway of the boathouse to stop his plunge forward onto the floor.

Adam caught the board, threw Rip an impatient glare, then returned his attention to Mike.

"Well," Mike said, running a leather-gloved hand over the half-finished hull of Ken's boat, "what do you think? Either of you interested?" He'd intentionally waited to approach them about buying the boat until the sun had passed beyond the large window at the front of the boathouse. Without the bright glare of sunlight on the old boat, it didn't look quite so disreputable. "I want to sell it and get it out of here before spring."

Adam turned apologetic blue eyes on Mike. "Sorry. I don't think so."

"But it just needs a little more work and it'll be seaworthy." Mike cringed at his exaggeration. If all it needed was a *little* more work, he'd have found the time to do it years ago—wouldn't he?

Problem was, it needed a whole lot of work, and Mike just didn't have the time to squander. Other things needed his attention. Important things. He tried not to think about the boat being a special project of Ken's. He tried not to feel guilty about getting rid of it.

"I understand that, Mike. I just don't have anywhere to use it but here, and it seems silly to buy a boat to use four weeks out of every year on a frozen lake." Adam exchanged sympathetic looks with Rip. "Have you asked any of the others?"

Mike sighed heavily and looked across the frozen lake. He'd talked to all of them and with the same results. "None of them want it, either."

"Why don't you put an ad in the newspaper. There's got to be someone around here who'll buy a boat." Rip stood the loose piece of lumber against the cradle brace.

The idea had occurred to Mike, but he'd rather the boat went to someone who had known Ken. Maybe then he could assuage this nagging feeling of betrayal. But after Peppy left last night, Mike had made up his mind to do something about his workload, and this boat was just one more thing in the clutter of his life he didn't need reminding him of what he had to do.

Too many other things really needed tending to for him to waste time worrying about expendable stuff—like refinishing a boat for sentimental reasons.

"It appears to me that you have three choices."

Rip had donned his Madison-Avenue persona. "You can refinish this relic and either use it or sell it. Or you can sell it as is. Or you can just tear it apart, scrap the lumber, then get on with your life." Rip started out the door, then paused. His tone terse and impatient, he added, "And were the choice mine, I'd scrap it."

Rip disappeared. Mike turned back to Adam. "What crawled into his underwear?"

A grin lit Adam's thin face. "I expect Rip's impatient to get back to his cot. Must be about time for his afternoon nap." He winked at Mike playfully. "He's only gotten in three or four hours today, and I expect that puts him behind schedule."

Mike looked down at his feet, where the snow from his boots had melted to form a small puddle, and chuckled softly. He glanced up to find Adam staring at him.

"What?"

Adam shook his head. "Nothing. It's just that I so seldom hear you laugh anymore. The sound surprised me."

"Laugh? Of course I laugh. I laugh all the time. I..." Mike let the thought drift away like smoke on a summer breeze. He gazed out across the frozen lake. The only time he could recall laughing lately had been with Jackie.

Adam was right. He had lost the ability to laugh. He'd stopped experiencing life, stopped seeing the lighter side of things, took himself too seriously. Hadn't he already decided that after Peppy left last night? Wasn't that why he'd decided to clear away some of the clutter? To sell Ken's boat?

"Adam, I..."

Mike found himself alone in the old building, except for the boat. Ken's boat. He considered Rip's suggestions.

"Refinish it or sell it?"

While doing a quick mental calculation on how much repairs would cost, Mike walked around the boat. The cost would drain money he couldn't afford to spend and time better spent elsewhere on important things.

"Sell it as is?"

Mike laughed. Who would buy a boat with a gaping hole in its side? He laughed again, but this time rancor replaced the humor.

Ken had bought the boat in exactly this condition. Mike ran his hand down the lap-strake siding and halted next to a gaping puncture in the hull. With his blunt fingernail, he chipped away at the dry rot eating into the neglected wood.

"Why didn't you fix this?" he asked his absent brother. "You always had to have things, then you left them."

Cautiously, he touched the windshield. It teetered in its frame, the cracked glass threatening to drop out at the least provocation. Inexplicable anger began building in his gut.

"You had no right to die and leave me with all this."

Perversely, he intentionally shook the boat and

watched the glass topple out of the frame, hit the floor and smash into millions of tiny shards.

"Damn it, you had no right to die." His voice rose.

The satisfaction he gleaned from his small act of vandalism, his small show of rebellion, pushed Mike further. Catching his fingers inside the edge of the hole in the hull, he yanked. The rotted wood splintered, then crumbled like dry crackers. He renewed his attack, this time grabbing the wood with both hands, then tearing it from the rusty nails holding it in place.

"You had no right," he repeated over and over, his voice echoing throughout the deserted boathouse.

When the wood no longer gave under his savage attack, he grabbed a hammer off the side bench to pry the lap-strake loose, ignoring the spots of blood where splinters ate at his skin.

Driven by an unseen force, he resumed his assault. With each board he wrenched from the hull, he enjoyed a new burst of freedom.

JACKIE LEFT the kitchen and headed for the lake. She needed to escape the confines of the four walls and the droning voices of the men finishing lunch. Normally, she ate with them, then cleaned the kitchen after they left, but today she didn't want company, only time to think.

As she neared the boathouse, the sound of crackling wood caught her attention. Drawn by curiosity, she eased inside the musty shed. The dim interior seemed even darker after coming in from the snow-bright landscape.

The boat shuddered, then settled back down into the wooden arms holding it. Beside it lay a pile of discarded lumber. She moved around the skeletal stern of the craft Adam had informed her had once belonged to Ken.

Mike had the claw end of a hammer wedged beneath a piece of the hull. He yanked sharply on the handle. The board popped loose. Grabbing the loose end, he levered it backward until it peeled away from the nails holding it to the hull ribbing.

He started, then glanced up at Jackie. He quickly looked away and began hammering the nails from the board. When the last nail surrendered, he tossed the plank on the growing pile.

She couldn't believe her eyes. "What are you doing?"

Mike wedged the claw under the next board and threw her an impatient look. "What's it look like? I'm junking this relic."

His stiff answer needled through her. She flinched. Were they back to being antagonists?

"I can see *what* you're doing. *Why* are you doing it? This was Ken's, right?"

"Yes."

"Adam said you were going to redo it."

He glanced at her, his gaze lingering on her face long enough to make her senses tingle.

"Adam was wrong."

"Wrong?"

"Yes, wrong."

Confused, she watched as he ripped another board from the hull. What had driven him to destroy something of Ken's?

She glanced up to find him studying her. Her heart throbbed heavily in her chest. She shifted her feet uncomfortably.

"I'm trying really hard to understand this, but so far I haven't understood a word since you said yes."

Resting his shoulder against the ruptured hull, he slowly plucked the fingers of his glove from his hand. "I'm sorting."

"Oh." *Well, that certainly cleared things up.* "Sorting?"

"Yup." His eyes held a new life, a sparkle she'd never seen there before. For some obscure reason, the sight made her want to weep with relief.

"I don't suppose you'd want to explain that."

"Nope."

At this point, Jackie didn't care why he was doing this, only that he was. The first step in cutting the threads that bound him to a dead man's dream. "Can I help?"

He stared at her a moment longer. He rolled his shoulders as if trying to remove kinks from the muscles. The worn material of his gray flannel shirt stretched across their thickness. A muscle bunched, then relaxed in his jaw. His hand tightened on the handle of the hammer, staining his knuckles white. "No. I gotta do this."

Jackie stepped behind him and watched while he pried another board loose.

Without warning, the rusty nailheads broke and released the board, propelling Mike backward into her, the momentum depositing both of them onto the stack of discarded lumber.

Not until she landed atop Mike's broad, flannel-covered chest did Jackie realize he'd somehow pivoted at the last minute to break her fall. She moved her hands cautiously against the fabric of his shirt. His muscles tensed beneath her touch.

So, Mr. Hamilton isn't quite as immune to me as he would like me to believe.

Inwardly, she grinned. Outwardly, she moved her legs in an attempt to free herself. Wedged between his, she couldn't go far, but the movement brought a sharp intake of breath from the man beneath her. The inner grin widened. Deliberately, she curtailed her efforts to rise.

Her warm breath fanned across Mike's face, heating the few parts of his body that weren't already at the boiling point. He gazed up into her blue eyes. Lord, he'd missed holding her, inhaling her special scent, hearing the musical sound of her laughter.

He placed his hands on her hips to move her off him before they both regretted what would happen if they remained as they were. She stared down at him. A faint smile curved her lips, tempting him beyond all reason.

"Damn you," he murmured, pulling her mouth down to his. "Damn you for making me want you."

When their mouths touched, Mike felt the parts of him that had died when he walked away from her come back to life.

Warm, soft and silky. Her breath sweet and seductive. Her body pliant, eager and ready. He could take her right here on the dirty boathouse floor and she wouldn't stop him. He knew that as surely as he knew that he wouldn't do it and as surely as he knew he'd regret for the rest of his life not doing it.

He broke the kiss.

"No."

He pushed her gently away, scrambled to his feet, then helped her to hers. He ran his hand through his hair, avoiding direct eye contact. "This is no good. No good," he repeated, then strode from the boathouse.

Jackie watched him go. He'd wanted that kiss as much as she had. What had stopped him? Would she ever learn the workings of his mind?

Looking around, she found an old nail keg and flopped down on it. She rested her elbow on her knee, then placed her chin in her hand and gazed out over the frozen lake.

Her toes began to absorb the cold, but she ignored them and concentrated on this latest meeting with Mike. The wind whistled through the gaps in the siding of the old structure, chilling her, but not as thoroughly as Mike's rejection had.

She'd about made up her mind that Mike thought he was protecting her from himself. It went along with what she already knew of him. Protecting others came as easily to Mike as breathing did for most people. It had started with Ken, then moved on to Land's End. The bird's nest. Shag. Mike never fished or hunted. He'd called Peppy's wife so she wouldn't worry about her husband. His pleasure at finding she'd let Old Silver Scales go. Mike's nature was to protect the things he cared about.

She brightened. Therein lay his flaw. *He did care about her.* She knew it. She could feel it in her pounding blood. That's why he was going to such extremes to protect her, even though it meant depriving himself. Now, when would he realize it?

Having lived with her father and brother for a number of years, she knew that reasoning things out and thinking them through was not a man's strong suit. That left her back at square one—nowhere.

"Well, damn it all, anyway—who asked him to protect me? Did I ever say I wanted him to protect me?" There were any number of things she wanted Mike to do to and for her, but protecting her from him wasn't one of them.

She kicked at a lump of snow that had fallen off her boot earlier. "It's that damn money. I just know it is. It stands between us like a big, ugly, green avenger."

She stood and paced the small space. How could she change Mike's mind? How could she convince him that her bank balance was a fraud, that she wasn't one of the Fortune 500? That except for a quirk of fate, she would still be living off the salary Dave paid

her and counting pennies. That Jacqueline Barrett and
Jackie Barrett were one and the same.

How, indeed? a little voice chided. *He'll never
know unless you tell him.*

But could she? Dared she?

Hadn't she just been thinking about Mike's need
to protect? Mike was probably one of the few people
in the world she could trust with her secret without
fear of his using it to hurt her. He'd never divulge her
secret. Why hadn't she thought about that long ago?

Now, all she had to do was find a way to convince
him the money could work for them—both of them—
and in so doing, reveal the real Jackie Barrett. To do
that, she'd have to get his undivided attention, and,
considering that he ran from her like the plague every
time she got near him, that wasn't going to be an easy
task.

THE NEXT DAY, after an aborted attempt at dinner the
night before to corner Mike in the kitchen and another
this morning, Jackie gazed forlornly out over the frozen lake. The gray sky hung low, threatening to dump
more snow on the mountains. The weather forecast
on Tommy's boom box that morning had predicted
possible blizzard conditions by nightfall.

Another icy rain from the previous night had transformed the surrounding forest into a glittering, dia-
mond-encrusted fantasy land. As the temperatures
rose above freezing and the ice melted, the hollow
crackle of the trees shedding their crystalline coats
echoed off the stillness. A piece of ice fell to a rock

and shattered, reminding Jackie how fragile happiness could be, how fleeting, how relative.

A few months ago, if anyone had asked her what would have made her happy, she would have said cooking. A month ago, the answer would have been to escape the repercussions of her lottery win. She'd managed to do both. She cooked on a daily basis for the men, and, if Harold's predictions were right about the plan she'd come up with in the fire tower, her financial quandary would soon be at an end—with Mike's cooperation. But neither accomplishment brought a smile to her lips. And she knew why.

Two long days and three endless nights had passed since she and Mike had made love. To her, it had seemed eons ago. In that time, Mike had avoided her like a case of the chicken pox.

She could have chalked the entire incident in the tower up to an overactive imagination, except for one thing—it had been all too real. Jackie had thought about the way Mike's hands felt against her naked flesh, relived it, endlessly.

The gulf between them gaped wider with each passing day. How could she stop it? No matter how she tried to head him off, Mike managed to elude her.

She wanted to tell him who she really was. And that kind of trust had come hard and with a lot of soul searching. Dave's unintentional betrayal, no matter how innocent, had affected her much more deeply than she'd admitted, even to herself. Once bitten, twice shy, her mother would have said.

But she did trust Mike now, and if he'd only listen,

she'd tell him everything, including her solution to the problems his brother had left him.

A sound behind her drew her from her deep thoughts. She turned to find a large buck and a doe standing just to her left. The buck moved; his slight limp identified him. Shag. Remembering how Mike remained statue still, she held her breath.

Shag nuzzled the doe's flank. She raised her head and turned away, as if uninterested. He nuzzled her again. This time, she walked a few feet from him and turned her large brown eyes toward Jackie. Jackie waited for the doe to bolt, but she didn't. Instead she stared, as if trying to communicate.

"Don't expect me to help," Jackie murmured. "I have my own man problems to find answers to."

A few minutes passed, and when Shag didn't approach the doe again, she seemed to take matters into her own hands and advanced on him. He turned away. She placed herself directly under his nose. He shook his head and trotted past her.

Men! They never know what they want. They throw out signals, then do exactly what you don't expect.

Undaunted, the doe followed, insinuating herself into Shag's line of vision, rubbing her head across his flank, then sidling up to him. With a snort, she walked slowly toward the tree line, glanced over her shoulder, then disappeared into the trees. Shag dipped his head, shook his antlers, then took off at a run after her.

Jackie smiled. *Smart lady. If you can't get what you want by honest means, then resort to seduction.*

Seduction! Of course. Why hadn't she thought of that?

She wasn't about to let a deer outdo her in the stalk-and-capture department.

Her spirits considerably lighter, she stood and looked toward the main lodge.

"Mr. Hamilton, hang on to your pants. You are about to come face-to-face with the Mata Hari of the Mountains." With a grin, she jogged off in the direction of the cabin to start her preparations.

BY THE TIME Jackie put her plan into action, the predicted blizzard had deposited three inches of fresh snow on Land's End. Accompanied by a wind-chill factor that would have sent Frosty the Snowman running for an electric blanket, the weather change made her trek to the main lodge a real challenge. Thank goodness she had a flawless sense of direction. Even with that, however, had she not covered this path many times in the past two weeks, the going would have been even rougher.

To make matters worse, the Arctic-born wind blew through her down parka and thermal underwear as if she had nothing on. Congratulating herself on deciding to wait until she reached the lodge to add the finishing touches to her perfumed, powdered and pampered body, she plowed on through the deepening white blanket. She clutched the small paper bag she carried tighter to her chest.

For once in his misguided life, Dave had screwed up in her favor. Not another person on the face of this planet would have included a skimpy, red lace teddy in a wardrobe intended for a month's vacation in a mountain fishing camp in the dead of winter. Only Dave.

But tonight it served Jackie's purpose perfectly— if she didn't catch pneumonia and die before she reached her objective. She shivered at the idea of exchanging her warm clothes for that scrap of lace, but the sacrifice and her ultimate victory far outweighed any discomfort.

Mike had to believe she was an accidental millionaire. To convince him, she needed his undivided attention. If looking like a bad imitation of a *Playboy* centerfold didn't get his attention, she didn't know what would. Even if it was with nothing more than hysterical laughter, she'd have him cornered and he'd have to listen.

Despite the chill wind and her bolstering thoughts, Jackie's cheeks warmed with embarrassment. She wasn't meant for this kind of stuff, this exposure, this total vulnerability. This could well turn into the most humiliating incident in her entire twenty-eight years.

Kicking that contingency aside, she ascended the lodge's broad front porch, then placed her hand firmly on the wrought-iron latch...and prayed. Mike never locked the door. If for some reason he'd changed his M.O., she would be in big trouble. She pressed on the thumb rest. The latch clicked, and with a gentle push, the heavy pine door swung inward. She sighed, stepped over the sill, then pushed the door closed.

The foyer lay in deep shadow, except for the red

glow of the dying embers in the lounge fireplace. The puny illumination barely afforded her enough light to get to the foot of the stairs. As she stepped on the first stair, the mantel clock chimed one. Jackie started, clutched the bag tighter and listened. Nothing.

Recalling from childhood, when she and her brother had sneaked into the house after curfew, Dave's revelation that staying off the center of the stair treads prevented unwanted squeaks, she snugged her shoulder against the wall. By the time she'd completed her noiseless ascent, then slipped into the bathroom to change clothes, her palms were moist and doubts had begun to buffet her mind.

What if he turned her away? What if the teddy didn't work its magic? What if he no longer found her attractive? What if... Oh, hell, she'd come this far, she couldn't chicken out now. Far too much depended on her success.

Sporting her daring outfit of seduction, Jackie stepped lightly from the bathroom in to the chilly hallway. Patting herself on the back for having enough foresight to case the joint, she took a deep breath and froze with her hand on the doorknob to Mike's room.

Her heart pumped like an out-of-control firehose. Goose bumps sprouted all over her exposed skin, which she figured constituted roughly about ninety-eight percent of her body. The cold pine floor turned her bare feet to ice.

Why couldn't men see an ankle-length, long-sleeved, flannel nighty and bunny slippers as sexy?

Why did looking sexy always include freezing one's buns off?

Ignoring the growing crop of goose bumps swelling her flesh, and bolstering her flagging courage with a deep breath, she turned the knob slowly, pushed the door open, then moved silently into the room.

Her cold skin soaked up the warmth from the fire blazing in the fireplace. The glow lengthened the shadows shrouding the big bed stationed directly in front of the hearth. She could see nothing but a large lump in the center of the mattress.

A new chill raced down her spine. What if Mike wasn't alone? What if he already had a bed companion? What would she do?

Simple. She'd wither and melt into the floorboards like the witch in that kid's story. Then she'd find a quiet, isolated cave in which to die of utter and complete humiliation.

She took a cautious step to the side of the bed, straining to see the occupant, or occupants, praying it would be the former and not the latter.

Suddenly, a large, strong hand captured her wrist in a viselike grip. She tried to scream, but her throat dried up. Her brain waves turned comatose.

The click of the door opening had roused Mike from his light slumber. Since he'd been dreaming about Jackie, finding her standing beside his bed didn't surprise him—at first. Then his groggy mind kicked into gear and registered the flesh-and-bone captive in his grasp.

"Jackie? What in the hell are you doing here?"

"Freezing, mostly."

He let go, flipped on the bedside lamp, then pushed himself to his elbow. The sight of her hit him with all the force of a runaway locomotive. His gaze traveled slowly over her alluring attire.

Red spaghetti straps prevented her lacy bodice from sliding off her cold-hardened nipples. A diamond-shaped piece of red silky material started at a point between and below her breasts, fanned out over her hips, then narrowed to the apex of her thighs. French-cut leg openings edged in more lace rode high on her pelvic bone, exposing the full length of her long, luscious legs.

He tore his gaze away and directed it at her face. The firelight haloed the fall of blond curls around her cheeks. Her blue eyes stared down at him with an expression that was half plea, half apprehension. Her even, white teeth worried her lush bottom lip.

She had never looked more beautiful, more appealing, more vulnerable—more off limits. *Send her back to her cabin—now!* But, as usual when it involved Jackie, his heart ignored his good sense.

Instead, love rose up in him, effectively cutting off his breathing. Each time he'd turned Jackie away, it had become increasingly more difficult. This time, it was impossible. Every nerve, every ounce of bone, muscle and sinew in his body cried out for this siren in red satin.

When it occurred to him why she'd appeared at his bedside, clad in about as much as a figment of his imagination, he smiled. She was trying to seduce him.

Didn't she know that wasn't necessary, that she'd already seduced him with her quick wit and her endless questions, with her sky-blue eyes and tempting smile? Didn't she know that he'd sell his soul to wake up every morning for the rest of his life with her in his bed?

And didn't she know that nothing in this lifetime was more impossible than allowing her to join him beneath the large patchwork quilt?

Chapter Eleven

Jackie snuggled deeper under the fluffy down patch-work quilt covering Mike's bed.

"That wasn't fair, you know."

Mike's voice came out of the darkness from where, after switching off the lamp, he'd isolated himself on the extreme far edge of the bed.

"What wasn't fair?" As if she couldn't guess.

"Prancing into my bedroom, half…not even half dressed, goose flesh blossoming on your hide like berries on a juniper bush, then shivering so hard your teeth chattered."

Guiltlessly, Jackie grinned into the semidarkness. "Okay, so the shivering and the teeth part were a bit much."

"Just a bit."

"But it did get your attention."

"That, combined with a few other things I just happened to notice." He shifted closer to the edge. "Just don't forget our deal. As soon as you get warmed up, you get your clothes on and leave. In the meantime, you stay over there, and I stay over here."

She rolled to her side, facing him. "You mean you're actually serious about sending me back out into the cold, dark night?" She injected just enough of a plaintive note into her voice to sound sexy—she hoped.

He groaned and scooted closer to his edge of the bed. The mattress dipped. "You got it. Just as soon as you stop shivering."

She'd stopped shivering the second she'd climbed beneath the down comforter and felt the heat emanating from him like a blast furnace. A fleeting image of the glimpse she'd gotten of Mike's naked torso dashed across her mind like a streaker at a pep rally.

The sound and the image brought on a new cascade of shivers, but this time, cold had nothing to do with their cause. She smothered a moan. Could she pull this off?

He obviously wasn't going to cooperate. And she'd never win her point if she didn't find a way to break through this wall he'd erected between them. She needed to feel comfortable in order to talk to him about herself and her plan. "Do you really hate having me here that much?"

Their breathing filled the silence.

"Mike?"

"I'm thinking."

Oh great! He has to think about it. So much for my big seduction scene.

Despair danced around her like the firelight shadows flitting over the ceiling. Jackie Barrett, hapless harlot, sorry siren.

"Well?"

Mike sighed heavily and rolled to face her, carefully balancing himself on the edge of the mattress. Having her here was temptation enough. If he made the mistake of touching her, he'd really be lost.

"No, Jackie. I don't hate having you here. I hate what I feel because you're here."

"What *do* you feel?"

Oh, no! She wasn't going to sucker him into a graphic discussion of his emotions, so they could lie here and watch his good sense fly out the window. He grinned into the darkness. Jackie had a way of doing that without crooking a finger. "Like I'm being seduced."

"Seduced?"

He smiled into the darkness. She sounded so innocent. But both of them knew innocence didn't come packaged in red silk.

"You think I came here to seduce you?"

Indignation. This was good. On top of being the most tempting bit of female flesh on this earth, the woman put on a damn good act, too.

"Didn't you?"

Jackie sat up. Cold air gusted under the covers. Mike grabbed a handful of comforter and pulled it around his shoulders.

"If you have to ask, I guess I blew it. If, indeed, that had been my intention," she qualified quickly. "This isn't exactly something you should have to take a vote on to decide." She dropped her voice to a soft, seductive purr. "Of course, I could always help you decide."

He didn't need any coaching to assess his body's reaction to her scanty attire. And if he didn't keep her from talking about how much he wanted her, she'd know, too. "Am I to assume that if I don't cooperate, you'll turn on your fatal charms?"

"You got it, buster."

She flopped down and, in doing so, moved closer. The mattress dipped. Helplessly, Mike rolled toward the middle. Jackie's foot curled around his calf and then slid up his leg. He gasped, scooted away, then clutched the mattress edge to prevent rolling down the incline her body weight had formed.

"We'll see who can be seduced and who can't," she announced in a cocksure tone.

"Whenever you feel ready to start." Mike swallowed hard, then rearranged the blanket and prayed she wouldn't push him to put his money where his mouth was. "You must be getting warmer by now," he croaked.

Jackie bit down hard on her lip. The slight huskiness in his voice told her she had him on the run. "How can I possibly get warm when you keep fanning the blankets?"

"Me?"

She could hear the smile in Mike's voice. Good, he wasn't angry at her. And, if he wasn't angry, she had a chance of convincing him to let her stay. And, if she got to stay, they could talk. Confidence began to push the insecurity from her mind.

"Are you sure you don't want to roll up a blanket and put it between us?"

"Should I?"

She snickered. "Only if you're afraid you can't control your male hormones."

"In case you forgot, *I* wasn't the one who invaded *your* bedroom. If anyone is having hormone-control problems, it's you." Suppressed laughter tinted his voice.

Teasing. Another good sign. She liked the Mike who teased. He reminded her of the man who rolled in the snow and threw pudding down her blouse—the man she'd fallen in love with, the man she could ask to share a dream.

"Speak for yourself, Hamilton. My hormones are doing quite nicely. Now, yours on the other hand..." She laid her cold hand on his bare thigh.

"Good grief!" He sat bolt upright and pushed her hand away. The quilt jerked to her waist. "Are you trying to freeze me?"

"You're the one who keeps stealing the covers." She hauled the quilt back up to her chin.

"My bed. My covers," he informed her smugly. He flopped back on the pillow, then pulled the quilt toward him, exposing her upper torso to the cool air of the room.

Goose flesh blossomed all over her body. "Didn't your mother ever teach you to share?" Grasping two handfuls of blanket, she dragged it in her direction.

In retaliation, Mike reclaimed the quilt with a sudden jerk. Refusing to relinquish her hold, Jackie found herself hauled along with the bed covering to his side of the bed.

She sprawled against his side, one leg over his, her arm trapped between them. Heat radiated from his skin and he smelled like wood smoke. His muscles, convulsing and rippling against her, stirred to life sensations that had her gasping for air. But he still made no move to escalate the situation into anything more.

Any normal man would have jumped her bones by now, but she had to get mixed up with a guy with a conscience. Damn his protective instincts! Her chances of seducing this stubborn man were going right down the toilet. If she didn't do something soon, she'd be right back out in the snow.

"Now, why didn't we think of this sooner?" she purred, running her free hand slowly over his bare chest, his rib cage, then precariously close to his swollen erection, before retracing the path.

He gasped and sucked in his stomach.

She grinned.

Mike had been restraining himself, but her words, her hands dancing over his flesh, her body sprawling over his, melted his composure as easily as ice cream on a hot summer day. He'd run out of mattress. He could do nothing but lie there and pray she'd lose interest. She didn't. Her hand began a new foray of his chest and rib cage. His tenuous grip on his physical reactions began to slip. He fisted his hands in the quilt.

Jackie squirmed closer, wrapping her leg around his.

He groaned and gripped the quilt tighter.

The arch of her foot slid sensuously along his bare calf.

Unable to stand any more, he placed his hands on her shoulder to force her back to her side of the bed. When his hands made contact with her silky skin, all thought of pushing her away vanished. Instead, he curled his hands around her arms and then lifted her onto his chest, pinning her solidly against him

Lord, but this woman had a startling effect on him. He always began any encounter with her with the best of intentions, but when he touched her, all his well-meaning plans went right out the window. And right now, fighting her off hovered far from what he wanted to do to Jackie Barrett.

He pulled her pliant body into his arms, then buried his face in the sweet-smelling cascade of blond curls splaying over his face.

"Are you warm yet?" he croaked.

"Past warm and approaching combustible."

His own temperature rose several degrees. Shock waves careened through Mike's body, numbing him to any lingering thought of removing her from his bed. Had he really wanted her gone? Had he really been ready to relinquish the completeness he always experienced in her arms? The answers came to him on a rush of emotion.

For the first time in years he admitted to needing another human being, but not just any human being. Good, bad or indifferent, he needed Jackie. He'd spent the better part of his life worrying about other people. First his mother, then Ken. Now, it was his turn.

Mike froze. The sensation started in the soles of his feet. A door had opened inside him, allowing a cool, refreshing, cleansing breeze to sweep through, clearing away the cobwebs around his heart. Then it grew hot and spread like a maverick forest fire, burning away the loneliness from his soul.

Foolishly, after Peppy had talked to him, Mike had believed that lightening his workload would bring him contentment and happiness. But he'd been wrong. Very wrong.

Only one thing, one person could do that. Jackie. Jackie and her love.

Running his hand over her back and down to her hip, he pressed his arousal into her soft thigh.

"Would you like me to help you cool off?"

She leaned back and peered down at him, grinning. "You have to learn to make up your mind. First you want me warmed up and now you want me cooled off."

He kissed her nose. "Correct me if I'm wrong, but weren't you the one who came in here hell-bent on seduction?"

She giggled. "Gee, and I thought I was being subtle."

"About as subtle as a forest fire." He rolled her beneath him and covered her mouth with his. He tasted again the sweetness of the woman who in a few short days had taught him how to live. This time, however, something new flavored her kiss—love.

Love as sweet and passionate as any he could ever ask for. Love for him.

He deepened the kiss. Jackie pulled away.

"I need to talk to you," she whispered breathlessly, then rested her forehead against his shoulder.

Talk he didn't need. What he *needed* was hidden beneath that slip of red lace. "Later," he mouthed against the throbbing base of her throat. "Much later, love."

His lips captured a silk-covered nipple. She gasped. With the echo of that one word reverberating in her heart, she slipped her arms around his shoulders and surrendered to the emotions rocketing through her body. Maybe now wasn't a good time to talk, after all.

Mike's warm hand encased her breast, massaging, molding. When the straps to the teddy slid from her shoulders in a slow sensuous motion, Jackie sucked in a deep breath. She knew what was coming. She knew, yet groaned aloud anyway, when Mike's mouth closed over her rock-hard nipple, then danced over her breast, scattering light kisses over her sensitized skin.

His hand moved to the swell of her hip, urging her body closer. She became acutely aware of Mike's nudity. A sheer scrap of red lace was the only barrier between his flesh and hers. She wanted it gone.

As if hearing her thoughts, Mike peeled the teddy down her body. His fingers traced over her skin, leaving quivering flesh in their wake. Then the teddy vanished and Jackie sighed with satisfaction. At last.

Mike rolled Jackie to her back. The mattress shifted, depositing them in an intimate tangle in the middle of the bed. This time Mike didn't fight the immediacy it perpetuated. Rather, he took full advantage and buried his face in the curve of her neck, then raised his mouth to her ear. He traced the outer rim with the tip of his tongue. A shudder started at her feet and pulsated through her body. Her nails dug into the flesh of his back.

Feeling this woman close to him, nestled in the curve of his body, Mike couldn't let her go. If he died tomorrow, he would die with Jackie in his arms. No matter what, Jackie was a part of him now, a part so essential to life that, if he did let go, he'd surely die. A familiar emotion welled up in him so strongly that he couldn't deny it, either to himself, or to Jackie.

"I love you," he whispered against her ear.

Jackie's emotions spun out of control. Her heart pounded as if it would leave her chest. Her head felt as light as thistledown. Her mind blanked out everything except Mike and his words. She wrapped her arms around him and held on, as if she feared he'd change his mind. She flung her leg over his and trapped him against her.

He loved her. Unconditionally. He didn't care if she was a millionaire or a pauper. He loved her. Mike Hamilton loved her. The words swirled round and round in her head. She wanted to shout it to the world.

Lottery be damned. Now, she was truly rich.

She longed to tell him that she loved him, too. But his mouth prevented further speech. His body slid over hers. With a groan of satisfaction, he entered her. She gave herself up to the sensation of being thoroughly loved by the man with whom she wanted to spend eternity.

Mike felt Jackie's elation in her response to him. That day in the tower had been something he thought never to experience again, but this, this went beyond all imagination. She gave, then gave more, until she had nothing left to give. And he took, greedily, driving deep into her warmth and languishing in the new sensations careening through him—contentment, happiness, love.

Certain he could stand no more, they reached the top of the passionate summit. And when he felt Jackie spasm around him, he let go, plummeting them over the edge together, spiraling down into a sea of feelings. For the first time in his life, Mike knew a completeness that came only with the unreserved giving and receiving of love.

JACKIE LAY CONTENTEDLY listening to the sound of Mike's even breathing, feeling against her cheek the steady rise and fall of his chest. Had she ever been this happy before in her life? She didn't think so. Mike loved her and she loved him. What more was there?

If she could only get him to agree to her plan for Land's End, they both could relax and revel in this newfound emotion.

"Mike?"

"Hmm?"

"We need to talk."

"Why?" His voice was deep and husky. He kissed the top of her head and squeezed her closer. "Don't need words. Unless you feel the need to proposition me again."

She turned her head and kissed his shoulder, knowing it would take very little for her to forget everything but Mike and his lovemaking. "All things in good time, you sex maniac." She propped herself on one elbow and looked down at him. His eyes were half closed, dreamy, sated. A tiny smile teased at his full mouth. "I love you. You believe that, don't you?"

He arched one dark eyebrow. "Yes. I believe you."

She leaned a little away, hoping the shadows would cloak any indecision showing in her face.

Silence engulfed them. The sound of the blizzard still howling outside drifted to them as if from another world, a world far separate from their cozy nest beneath the goose-down comforter. The faint aroma of wood smoke, mixed with the fragrance of their lovemaking, hung in the air.

When Mike made no attempt to probe for what was bothering her, Jackie lay back down, feeling his barriers slipping into place. Unfortunately, his innate ability to protect included himself.

"I want to talk about Land's End," she said quickly, before her nerve deserted her or before his barriers got insurmountable. She waited to see if he'd say anything. Nothing. She forged on. "I've been talking with Harold and we've worked out a plan that will get the camp on its feet, both financially and physically.''

His body stiffened. "Oh?"

She dearly wished she'd never started this, but it was too late to pull out now.

"If you let me invest in fixing up the camp, we can turn it into a retreat for inner-city kids and their families.''

Mike remained silent. Jackie's discomfort grew.

"I talked to Tony and he said he used to come to the mountains when he was a child with a group called the Fresh-Air Fund. I got to thinking about Tony wanting to bring his family, but he couldn't.'' She paused. "Oh, Mike, can't you just see it? All those families, together, learning about nature, breathing unpolluted air....'' She wasn't doing a good job of this. "Anyway, with our—''

"Hold it." Mike pushed her from him and sat up. "Who gave you the okay to make all these plans without consulting me?''

His voice was as rough as coarse sandpaper. She cringed. "I didn't want to tell you about it until we had it all mapped out.''

"Didn't it occur to you that I might like the camp just the way it is? The way Ken wanted it to be?''

That did it. The man was too stubborn for his own good. "Damn it, Mike, when are you going to stop finishing everything for your brother?''

He crossed his arms over his chest and glared at

her, one dark eyebrow elevated. "What the hell is that supposed to mean?"

"Exactly what I said. You've taken on finishing this camp, not because it's what you want, but because it's what Ken wanted. Well, how do you know it is what Ken wanted? How do you know if he'd lived he would still want it? Or would he have tired of it like all the other projects that are half started around here?"

Jackie could have torn out her tongue. She'd never meant to attack his brother, but she couldn't stand seeing him continue this idea he had that he was responsible for Ken.

"Just who the hell are you to know anything about Ken? He was my brother. I knew him better than anyone."

"Yes, you did. And if you're totally honest with yourself for a change, you'll admit that the chances are very good that he would have lost interest in this place long ago." Jackie sat up and clutched the comforter under her chin. Arguing without a stitch of clothing on certainly undermined your confidence.

"Why don't you mind your own business?"

The words cut as if tiny shards of glass had embedded themselves in her heart. "I love you. I hate seeing you do this to yourself. You need your own dream. That makes this my business."

"Loving me doesn't give you the right to tell me how to run my life."

"Why not? Loving Ken gave him the right to tell you how to run it."

The room went stone silent. Only their labored breathing and the crackle of the dying fire filled the gap of endless tension looming between them.

Mike left the bed. He picked up his discarded jeans, then slipped them on. Without looking at her, he squatted before the fireplace and began feeding wood into the glowing embers coating the bottom of the firebox. Slowly, and deliberately, he built the stack of logs, then blew on the coals until the fire flashed and ignited the dry timber.

Jackie watched silently from the bed. She'd trespassed on forbidden territory by attacking Ken. Even knowing that, she could not retract the words. Mike needed to hear them, needed to start living his life for himself. What was going on in his mind?

"Is that why you came here tonight, all sexy and seductive? Is that what this whole show was about?"

Jackie started. "What?"

"Didn't you come here figuring that if you got me to take you into my bed, you could talk me into going along with your plan?"

He didn't turn around, just continued to fuss with the fire, rearranging the logs he'd just, moments earlier, stacked with such care.

As her heart shattered into tiny pieces, Jackie lowered her feet to the cold floor. That had been part of her reason for coming, but there was so much more that he couldn't—wouldn't—see.

"Whatever you believe, the truth is that I came here for the reason you stated and because I love you and I couldn't go on with this gap between us. I want to help. I have the money and I thought—''

Mike stood abruptly and swung on her. His expression blazed with fury. ''That's what it all boils down to, right? You have the money and I don't. You have the money and can buy whatever you little heart desires, including me. Well, I'm not more for sale any more than this camp is.''

Too stunned to rebut his accusations, she could only gape at his unreadable face silhouetted by the fire glow. She didn't need to see his expression. His tone of voice said it all. She deliberated explaining about her lottery win, but considering his reaction to her plan for the camp and what he'd just said about her buying him, she vetoed the idea. One bombshell an evening was enough for anybody, even her.

For a moment, he continued to glare at her, then turned away. He leaned his forearm on the mantel and rested his head on it. ''Leave, Jackie. Leave now before we hurt each other more.''

He couldn't hurt her more. The pain started deep inside her and spread like a canker, inflicting an agony she could barely tolerate without crying out. She'd reached out to help and, instead, had driven him away.

Wordlessly, Jackie rose, picked up the discarded teddy, then left the room. Frigid air still hung in the hall, but the chill couldn't compete with the cold that had seeped into her heart and soul.

Moments later, dressed and wanting to outrun the

pain building inside her, Jackie hurried down the stairs, then out into the swirling, blinding wall of white.

Chapter Twelve

Mike walked slowly down the stairs to the foyer of the lodge. The breaking light of dawn slivered weakly through the dark shadows. The room was deathly quiet. Jackie had been gone for some time. He'd waited intentionally to be sure of that. Facing her right now, after the stupid display of temper he'd just put on, rated very low on his to-do list. He could kick himself. He should have at least listened to what she had to say.

Today, after they'd both had time to calm down, he'd find her and apologize, then let her explain. He'd also try to make her see why he'd flown off the handle at her.

The chill of the big empty building crept into his body. He shivered, then pulled his flannel shirt closed and secured the buttons. But the coldness encasing his heart remained.

Deep down, he knew Jackie wouldn't seduce him to get what she wanted, any more than she would use her money to get her hands on Land's End. What had prompted him to make such asinine statements? He didn't have to search long or far to find answers.

Jackie had accomplished something he couldn't. She'd found a way to save Land's End.

The truth of that had delivered a bruising blow to the breadbasket of his almighty male ego. After he'd spent five years scraping money together, juggling the books like an inept circus performer, doing makeshift repairs to the camp and groveling in bank presidents' offices, she'd waltzed in here and solved the problem with a flick of her checkbook, and asked for nothing in return. He should be grateful, not tearing into her like some dog who'd lost his bone.

But had she really solved the problem? Her solution in no way resembled what Ken had intended for the camp. And hadn't he sworn to make the camp what Ken had envisioned? But what exactly *had* Ken envisioned? Was it more Mike's own vision?

Her accusing words came back to him with stinging force.

"When are you going to stop finishing everything for your brother?"

He plowed his fingers through his hair and wandered over to the reception desk. For a moment, he argued with himself about whether to turn on the small desk lamp, then decided a little illumination might be good for his soul—in more ways than one—and clicked on the lamp.

The weak light splashed across the glossy patina of the desk—yet another project Ken had started and Mike had finished for him.

Mike ran his fingertips over the satiny surface, vividly recalling how he'd labored for days, sanding, buffing, then sanding again and buffing some more, before coating the wood with a thick layer of varnish. Ken had never gotten past adding it to the growing list of things to be done—things that never got done, unless Mike did them.

As much as he hated to admit it, Jackie had been right on target. He'd made Ken's life easy by mopping up after him from the time their father had walked out on his family until the day Ken died.

No. Ken's death hadn't put an end to it. Mike was still doing it. Still finishing up Ken's projects, from that boat to the camp itself.

Ken had always acted irresponsibly, as irresponsibly as the woman driving the car. Mike had condoned his brother's behavior by consistently being there to pick up the pieces and see things through to the end. It had been apparent in so many aspects of their lives. Even with Shag. Ken had seen the deer as a momentary distraction. Mike had loved Shag and taught him to survive—something he'd never taught Ken.

Mike had always been the sensible one, the one unwilling *not* to do the right thing, the one who never acted without thinking. Frivolous and impetuous were foreign words to Mike. As a result, he'd built himself a prison.

Why didn't I see that?

He looked around him. Resentment took root in his thoughts and flourished like a fertilized weed. The only joy and freedom he'd known in the past five years had come to him in the days since Jackie had become a part of his life. Why? Because she'd shown him how to be himself and not walk in the shadow of another man.

Lowering his head to his hands, he came as close to weeping as he ever had in his life. Later might be too late to make amends with Jackie. He had to get a hold on his emotions and find Jackie sooner. But before he could do that, he had to come to terms with himself.

In a desperate attempt to clear away the pain and confusion battering his mind, he grabbed the stack of unopened mail he'd been ignoring for days. Slowly, he shuffled through the pile, half reading the return addresses on each envelope.

One caught his attention.

Why would the bank be sending him a letter? He hadn't applied for another loan yet. He ripped the envelope open, deciding it had to be some additional papers confirming the denial of the second mortgage application he'd received days ago.

Unfolding the paper, he caught the check that fell out moments before it fluttered to the floor. Quickly, he scanned the letter. It was the first installment on the second mortgage. They'd changed their minds.

After reassessing his application at the bank president's request, they'd decided to grant the loan. It would be issued in segments, as he made improvements to the camp. If at any time the bank felt the camp wouldn't make it, the loan would be terminated.

He crumpled the paper in his hand. He should have

been celebrating, but he could feel only despair. Now that he had the means to do it, saving Land's End no longer mattered. What mattered was saving Mike Hamilton.

It occurred to him at that moment that he'd been fighting to preserve something he didn't even believe in, something that, as Jackie had pointed out, was someone else's dream. In actuality, he hated the very thing the camp advocated, killing animals.

Ken loved hunting and fishing, so it seemed natural for him to buy the camp. Mike had gone along with it out of love for his brother and the sheer habit of doing things Ken's way. And in going along with it, he given up his own dream of entering the Forestry Service and protecting the very things Ken had sought to destroy.

When the door flew open and admitted seven very upset men, he had no idea how long he'd been standing there clutching the crumpled letter.

"Is she here?" Peppy's voice grated with concern.

His demanding tone took Mike off guard. "Who?"

"Jackie. Is she here?" This time Adam stepped forward with the question.

"No." The implications of the question struck Mike full in the face. "Isn't she at the cabin?"

The men looked at one another, none seeming to be too eager to answer Mike.

Impatient and suddenly filled with a cold dread, Mike grabbed Tony's jacketsleeve. "Isn't she at the cabin?" Fear giving way to panic elevated the tone of his voice.

Tony shook his head. "Her bed hasn't been slept in."

"The covers weren't even messed up," Tommy added.

As Mike released the fabric, Tony staggered backward and caught himself on the edge of the desk.

"She was here last night," he heard himself explaining through a fog of torment. "We fought and she ran out, but I thought she went back to the cabin."

Oblivious to everything else, Mike raised his worried gaze to the swirling snow coming through the gaping door. The blizzard had ended shortly before dawn, but the wind gusts drifted the snow, covering any footprints that might help them track Jackie.

"Mike." The tips of Doc's fingers curled into Mike's arm, the biting pressure belying the calmness of the old man's tone. "We have to find her."

Roused from his thoughts of Jackie wandering aimlessly through the white storm, he hurried toward the storage room at the back of the lounge. Throwing open the door, he began hauling out the snowshoes and flare guns he, a member of the local rescue team, stored at the camp.

Handing the guns to each man, he pointed at the snowshoes. "Each one of you take a pair. You'll need them to get through the drifts." He fought the tormenting visions that buffeted his mind and kept himself focused on organizing the search party. "We'll fan out in a half circle. Stay within sight of the man to your left and right. Adam, you take one end and I'll take the other.''

''Shouldn't we call someone to help?'' Tommy hovered near the phone, his young face older with worry. Moisture made his eyes glitter. He wiped at them with his gloved hand.

They didn't have time to wait for the mountain rescue team to show up, but Tommy needed to be doing something to assure himself everything was being done that could be.

''Call 911. Tell them what's happened and to send out the rescue team. You stay here and man the phone. When they come, show them which way we went.'' Mike's instructions put a little starch in the boy's drooping shoulders.

Tommy nodded. ''Kim will be here soon. I'll have her make coffee and sandwiches.''

Mike smiled and patted the boy's shoulder. ''Thanks.'' He grabbed a pair of snowshoes for himself and then headed toward the door, shoving his flare gun in the pocket of his down jacket. ''Let's go,'' he called to the rest of the men. ''The more that snow blows, the harder it's gonna be to find any tracks.''

''Mike?''

Tommy's voice stopped Mike's headlong rush. He glanced over his shoulder at the kid.

''Find her?''

Words stuck in Mike's throat. Forcing a reassuring half smile, Mike gave the boy a succinct nod, then dashed through the door into the sea of white.

"JACKIE!"

Mike's voice echoed back to him from the stillness surrounding the small gathering of men. Silence answered. The deadening silence that always accompanies a snowfall.

"Jackie!"

More silence.

"Jackie!"

Mike swallowed hard against the rawness in his throat, a residual effect of calling her name over and over for an hour. So far, they'd found nothing—not a footprint or a broken branch. Nothing. He didn't have to tell the six men what this meant. He could read it in their faces.

Over a foot of snow had fallen during the night and the wind had drifted it into piles that sometimes threatened to swallow his six-foot body. She could be anywhere, including buried beneath one of those mountains of snow they'd passed.

His legs ached from dragging the heavy snowshoes through drift after drift, but the distress building steadily to desperation inside him drove him relentlessly on. His toes were numb. The bitter cold had robbed all feeling from his fingers long ago. He worked them inside his gloves to boost the circulation.

"Mike."

A hand halted his forward movement. He pivoted to find Adam standing beside him, the others gathered in a silent half circle. They reminded Mike of mourners gathered around a grave site.

"Why are we stopping?" Mike knew what panic could do in a situation like this, and he was trying his damnedest not to let it overcome him. He'd been on plenty of searches for lost hikers. He knew the rules. Stay clearheaded and focused. But none of those hikers had been out there because of his stupidity. And none of them had been Jackie.

"Need...to...rest a...moment." Adam choked out the words around gasps for air.

Fear for the woman he loved prompted Mike to argue, then he looked at the others. Rip, used to sitting behind a desk and topping out his exercise program by chasing a cab down Madison Avenue, leaned against a tree, head lowered, trying to even out his breathing. Doc's face glowed cherry red and not entirely from the cold wind. Tony jogged in place, rubbing his hands together to warm them. Harold had sunk to the ground next to another tree, his bulky jacket front rising and falling rapidly. Even the stalwart Peppy showed signs of exhaustion.

These guys didn't have the stamina for this kind of exercise. He should have considered that, but all he'd been able to think about was Jackie, Jackie out there somewhere, Jackie maybe...

"Maybe we should go back and check the lodge." The halfhearted suggestion came from Rip, who now danced in place and rubbed his gloved hands together.

Mike looked from one tired face to the next. "You all go on back. I'm going to keep looking. Tell the rescue team where we've looked and where I am.

They should be at the lodge by the time you get there.''

Adam caught Mike's sleeve. "I'm staying."

One by one, they all echoed Adam's decision. Mike looked at their determined faces and wondered if any woman other than Jackie had so completely and totally won the hearts of eight men. There wasn't a man among them who would not gladly lay his life on the line to ensure her safety.

"Thanks." His voice sounded as raspy as his throat felt. He swallowed hard and drew a deep breath. "Okay, then we need to organize this a little better. We'll split up into teams of two. We can cover more ground that way." He didn't add that they could all move at their own speed that way and not overtire themselves. "I'll go alone, since I know these mountains better than any of you. If you find her, fire one flare." He tilted his head back and checked the sky. Thank goodness the wind had died to a whisper and visibility had improved. Hope rose up, invigorating him and renewing his determination. "We shouldn't have any trouble spotting it."

The men chose their directions and left the clearing in their assigned pairs, leaving Mike behind, trying to gather his thoughts. "Come on, Hamilton. You're not a greenhorn. You've done this before. Where would she be?"

Forget about using your head for a change, Hamilton, and follow your heart, a little voice inside him prompted.

He raised his head and scanned the trees. The fire

tower. Without questioning the logic of his decision, he took off through the trees. If he allowed his usual common-sense thinking to invade his thoughts, he'd have considered the chances of Jackie reaching the tower in a blinding snowstorm and altered his destination. But logical thinking hadn't gotten him very far with Jackie.

After having walked for a few minutes. He slowed his pace to closely inspect the lower limbs of some evergreens. Odd. They held an accumulation of snow, but not nearly as much as the limbs around them. Almost as if someone had pushed them aside, dislodging them and relieving them of the biggest share of their burden. He checked for tracks. None.

From all indications, the wind had been northerly all night. Mike moved around the tree to the south side. While deep drifts had collected on the north side, on the south side the snow barely covered the frame of the snowshoe. If Jackie had come this way, she would have skirted the higher drifts and stayed to the south of the trees where it was easier walking— if she could have even seen where she was walking.

Carefully he moved along, studying the ground as he went for signs—any signs—that she'd passed this way. Even though his heart pushed him on, his head still had influence over his logic. Not far down the trail, he found what looked like nearly obliterated scuff marks in the snow, as if someone had fallen or slipped. He looked around for more signs, but found nothing.

About to push on, he glanced at the trunk of the

dead pine next to him. Where the snow had been blown against the bark, it had stuck. In the middle of that cap of snow was a small mitten-shaped print.

Jackie!

Happiness crowded out the despair from his heart. Shocked to find his vision blurred, he looked in the direction of the tower. Blotting out all thought except finding her alive and well, he roughly wiped the moisture from his cold cheeks and plowed on, his gaze fixed on a distant spot. Not until he saw the tower rising behind a snow-clad hill did he shift his focus and allow himself to think.

"Jackie."

Her name slipped from his frigid lips. He craned his neck to see the little building at the top. She was there. His heart told him so. Drawing the flare gun from his pocket, he fired it toward the blue sky, then kicked off the snowshoes.

Nearly falling several times on the snow-slick rungs of the metal ladder during his hasty ascent, he paused on the narrow platform encircling the tower room. He held his breath and opened the door with a gentle shove.

His gaze went to her, as if drawn by an invisible magnet. Only then did the dread that had propelled him through the drifts of snow for the past couple of hours vanish. In its place flowed sweet relief.

Jackie lay on her back on the cot, her hands resting at her waist outside the blanket covering her, her eyes closed, her body deathly still. When he saw the faint rise and fall of the blanket over her chest, he wanted to shout with joy.

Instead, he moved to her side, half aware of the warmth from the little space heater and the clothes draped around the room drying. Despite the ordeal of the past few hours, or maybe because of it, he chuckled softly. Resourceful for a city gal.

Careful not to disturb her, he eased down to the side of the cot. For a time, while his heart regained its natural rhythm, he studied her face in sleep. He brushed aside a wisp of hair that had gotten tangled in her long lashes.

What an exquisite woman. Just looking at her made him ache with love for her.

Following an instinct as natural as awakening to a new day, he bent and brushed a soft kiss against her lips. Her eyelids fluttered, then her eyes opened wide. Instantly, she bathed him in a brilliant smile.

"I knew you'd find me."

Her whispered words wrenched at his heart. She always seemed to have more faith in him than he had in himself. Too overcome to do or say anything, he gathered her to him, nestling her securely against his chest. In that instant, when she smiled at him, Mike knew he'd never let her go again.

The problems they'd have to surmount to build a life together seemed small and inconsequential compared with what they'd be losing if they didn't try. Later. There would be plenty of time for combing through that tangle later. Right now, Mike wanted to hold Jackie and savor the rightness of her in his arms.

He suddenly understood what Peppy meant about sorting through the clutter of life. Material things came and went, but love, pure love, came once in a lifetime, and the smart guy knew the difference and hung on to what counted—forever.

He tightened his embrace and smiled into her hair.

Jackie languished in a sensation she'd thought never to experience again—the security of being in Mike's arms. The aroma of fresh air clung to his hair and clothes. She inhaled deeply. The essence of Mike. She'd never again feel a breeze caress her cheeks or see a wildflower bloom without thinking of this man. Truly Mother Nature's son.

Last night had been a nightmare, and not just because of the howling storm that had caused her to wander aimlessly through a blinding wall of white nothingness. Finding the tower had been a stroke of luck. Maybe her guardian angel working overtime. Whatever, or whoever, had guided her footsteps would remain a mystery to her.

When she'd run out of the lodge, she'd been certain her impetuous offer to finance Land's End had killed anything between them. But now, with him holding her as if he'd never let her go, she allowed herself to hope otherwise.

Lying here alone last night, listening to the storm raging outside in time with the one raging inside her, she'd had plenty of time to think. She leaned away to look at him.

"Mike, I had no right to say all those things about

Ken and you. God knows, if it had been Dave and me, I'd have probably done the same thing.''

"Shh." He covered her lips with his finger. "Don't talk. Not yet. Just let me hold you."

She wanted to add that she still believed he'd shackled himself to another man's dream and that no matter how much he loved his brother, he had to let go for his own good. When she tried to tell him just that, he replaced his fingers with his mouth. His lips conveyed such intense poignancy that she had to fight to restrain a sob of happiness. If only it could be like this forever.

But it couldn't. She knew that in her heart. Not until they got things settled between them, namely Land's End and Ken. But as long as he held her, she couldn't think coherently.

She gently pushed herself from his embrace, scooted around him, then rose from the cot, dragging the blanket with her for covering.

"We need to talk about what happened last night, what we said." She glanced at his face for his reaction, since he hadn't made a sound, and knew in her gut that once more the specter of Ken and Land's End stood between them like an impenetrable stone fortress.

As she gathered her clothes, she clutched the blanket closer, more to cover her vulnerability than her body.

"Don't feel you have to get dressed on my account. I can give you at least one very good reason not to," Mike said, his voice ringing with forced humor.

Any other time, his suggestive comments would have sung through her blood and his teasing would have made her smile, but not now. She swallowed a sob and fought the craving to drop the clothes, run back into the shelter of his arms and beg him to make love to her until the world faded away.

"That's not the answer," she said, as much for her own benefit as for his. Slowly, she began to get dressed.

"I wasn't aware we were looking for any."

She glanced his way. He stood and hooked his thumbs in the belt loops of his jeans. His broad chest strained against the buttons of his plaid shirt. He was the most magnificent creature she had ever seen—and the most pigheaded.

"That's part of the problem. You're so sure you have all the answers already that when someone else offers a new one, you turn them away."

He took a step toward her. "Jackie, what's wrong? If it's last night…"

"Mike!"

Doc's voice echoed up to them from below the tower.

Jackie glanced at the windows, then back to Mike. "How did he know?"

"I imagine they're all down there. After I found you, I sent up a flare so they'd stop looking. They must have followed the direction," he said offhandedly. "Jackie…"

"We'd better go. They're waiting." Pulling on her parka and mittens, she moved toward the door.

Suddenly, Mike's body blocked her path. "Not until you talk to me."

For a long moment, her gaze searched his face. "Will you let me finance the repairs of Land's End?" She waited. Mixed emotions chased across his rugged face.

Finally, he shook his head. "No."

Jackie exhaled a painful breath. "Then I guess there's nothing more to talk about."

She sidestepped his large body, then slipped out the door, trying her best to hide the fact that he'd just shattered what was left of her world.

Packed snow made the platform slick. She picked her way to the top of the ladder and looked down. Six beaming faces shone up at her.

"Jackie! Thank God you're all right!" Adam called up.

She returned their smiles, but inside she cried. Was she all right? Would she ever be all right again?

Chapter Thirteen

"Do you have to leave?" Tommy did nothing to veil the plea behind his words.

Jackie put the last of her clothes into the suitcase, closed the lid, then snapped the locks into place. Turning, she met the imploring look of the young man hovering in the opening of her makeshift bedroom.

"Yes."

"But you still have time before the end of the month."

"I know. But I have to leave now."

"Why?" The perennial question of the young.

"It's better that I don't wait."

She couldn't explain her reasons to this teenager. Hell, she couldn't explain them to herself. All she knew for sure was that she had to get out, away from here, away from...

"Will you write or something?"

"You'll be gone soon, too, in a few days. Where will I send my letters?"

From the pocket of his fashionably torn jeans, he extracted a folded sheet of yellow legal paper. He extended it to her. "We all put our names and addresses on here for you. So you could keep in touch."

"Thanks." The gesture warmed her, but it couldn't entirely erase the loneliness encasing her heart.

"Maybe you could come back next year." His normally bright brown eyes, dulled by disappointment, glimmered with hope.

She hated to be the one to kill it again. "No. I don't think I'll be coming back to Land's End...ever."

How could she come back? How could she bear to see Mike laboring under the burden he'd chosen to carry? Wasn't that why she'd decided to leave? Because watching him continue his fruitless efforts to preserve and protect something that rightfully belonged to his brother, becoming more and more bitter as time went on, would be more than her heart could stand?

"It's Mike, isn't it?" Tommy spoke with such vehemence that it startled Jackie.

"No. You can't blame this on Mike. This was my decision. Mike had nothing to do with it."

Thank goodness, the boy seemed to grudgingly accept that. With all his other worries, Mike didn't need this young kid attacking him about this.

She tucked the folded paper carefully in the pocket of her jacket. "I'll write to all of you. That's a promise." She smiled past the tears burning at the back of her eyes. "You guys are like family to me now. I could never just forget you."

The boy's face brightened some. He blinked several times, then cleared his throat and straightened his spine.

"Did you bring the car down from the lot?"

He nodded.

"Would you put these bags in the trunk for me?"

"Sure." He grabbed the suitcase handles. "By the way, Mike's truck was gone." He shrugged his shoulders. "Thought you'd like to know."

She kissed his cheek. His ears glowed bright pink. "Thanks."

It hurt like blazes that she wouldn't see Mike again and that he hadn't come to say goodbye, but, all in all, it was better this way. Stepping back, she allowed Tommy to swing the suitcases to the floor. She waited until he'd gone, then sank down on the edge of the bed. Her hand came in contact with something soft and silky. Without looking down, knowing what she touched, she curled her fingers into the fabric of the red lace teddy.

She hadn't packed it intentionally. She had enough painful memories to carry home with her. She needed no further reminders. Shoving the garment into the brown paper bag she'd used for trash, she turned her back on it, then left the alcove, forcing a smile to her numb lips for the benefit of the six men gathered around the table.

Their gazes followed her approach, each man exhibiting his own version of regret and sadness. How she dreaded leaving them. She hadn't lied to Tommy. They were, indeed, like family. Each of them had carved his own little notch in her heart and all seven of those dear faces would remain in her memory forever.

"Coffee?" Doc raised the pot in his customary gesture of invitation.

She nodded, not trusting her voice quite enough to speak, and not quite as anxious to leave as she had been. Sliding into a chair between Peppy and Harold, Jackie looked at the two men flanking her. Neither of them looked up from the coffee they swirled absently in their mugs. When she checked out the others, they were all working just as diligently at occupying themselves.

Rip, wide awake for once, polished the handle on his coffee spoon with his napkin. Doc had removed his glasses and, using his thumb and forefinger, applied pressure to the bridge of his nose, as if it ached. Tony had left the group and stared out the window.

Adam. Dear, dear Adam. Of all of them, Adam was the one it hurt the most to leave. He pulled out a white handkerchief, wiped surreptitiously at his eyes, then blew his nose noisily.

"Damn cold," he mumbled and shoved the handkerchief into his back pocket. Glancing at her, he sent her a liquid grin, then he, too, took to swirling the contents of his mug and studying it in depth.

"Oh, goodness. Who'll cook?" Harold's troubled voice broke the silence.

Five heads swiveled toward him. Five faces glowered at him.

"Do you ever think of anything but your stomach and your numbers?" Peppy snapped. But, somehow, even with his best scowl in place, his tone lacked its usual censure, as if all the starch had drained out of him.

Harold mumbled an apology and dipped his head.

"All right, you guys, enough of this." Jackie pushed herself to her feet and jammed her hands on her hips like a mother about to scold her brood. "I'm not disappearing from the face of the earth. I'll write. I'll even visit. Tommy gave me your addresses. And you all know where to find me." She patted Harold's shoulder. "You come see me at the restaurant and I'll make you the best meal you've ever had."

"I'll be by. You can count on it, but you don't have to feed me. I'll just be happy to see you."

Harold refusing food? This was more serious than she'd thought. She had to get out of here before they all collapsed into a sobbing pile of humanity.

"Good. That invitation goes for all of you. Now, come on, smile and walk me to my car."

Standing, almost in unison, they dutifully plastered smiles on their faces, then followed her out the door.

Not eager to prolong the goodbyes, she quickly hugged and kissed each in turn, then climbed into the driver's seat of her low-slung red Porsche. Before she could start the engine, a light tapping on the driver's window drew her gaze to Tommy's face peering in at her. She cranked the window down.

"I wanted to say thanks for the...the...well, you know."

She didn't need him to tell her he referred to his crush on her. She patted his hand where it rested on the door. "You just take care. Let me know how medical school goes." She smiled. "And, Tommy, promise me you'll never lose sight of your dreams."

He nodded mutely, then sniffed and turned away.

Moisture threatened to blur her vision. She blinked it away. Tears always seemed to be hovering so close to the surface lately—most annoying to a woman who never cried.

The car's powerful engine roared to life with the twist of the key. Jackie glanced once more at the circle of dear faces. Before she could shift into gear, a large white Dodge Charger skidded to a halt, effectively blocking her path.

As she watched, Mike emerged from the pickup. His face wore the same expression it had the day he'd spotted her luggage—implacable.

Please, don't make this any harder for me. Just let me leave quietly.

Mindlessly, she drank in the sight of his hard muscular legs gloved in tight denim, the sun glinting off the blue highlights in his hair, his sensual mouth drawn into a tight, determined line and those black, luminous eyes burning right through the windshield and into her heart.

He tromped around the hood of the car to her door. Before she could crank the window up, he reached through it, turned off the ignition, then yanked out the keys.

"What are you doing?"

Ignoring her hot protest, he balled his hand around

the keys, reared back and then tossed them into the trees.

"Are you nuts?"

"I'm being decisive, Ms. Barrett. I'm taking charge of my life. Doing a little housecleaning. Now, if you'd please get out of the car so we can talk...." He stepped back to give her room to open the door.

When she didn't, he opened it for her. She grabbed the handle and pulled it closed again. He glared at her. "Don't try my patience."

Try *his* patience? "Why you big—" She sputtered, searching for words. Before she could find them, Tommy raced up to the car.

"Jackie, thank goodness you aren't gone yet. You forgot this." He extended a hand holding the red lace teddy.

She snatched it from him, then tempered the action with a smile. "Thank you, Tommy."

"You're welcome. I knew it wasn't in the trash on purpose. Must have slid off your bed or something."

Something told Jackie this news wasn't going to sit well with Mike. She sneaked a peek at him. Lips drawn into a line of suppressed anger, he stared down at the scrap of nightwear and frowned darkly. "You threw it away?"

Casting a quick glance at the seven faces grinning at them, she glared back at him. "I don't see that what I do with my clothing is any concern of yours."

"Oh, you don't?"

"No."

"Well, let me enlighten you. That happens to be

the piece of clothing you had on the last night I made love with you. So if you don't want it, I do." He snatched it from her fingers.

"I didn't say I didn't want it." She snatched it back.

"Then why did you throw it away?"

She remained silent. "Well?" Still no answer. "Could it be because it reminded you of the man you were about to desert?"

"Desert? Now, just one minute, Mike Hamilton." She stopped her protest short, knowing that was exactly why she'd thrown it away, but unwilling to admit that to him. "What would you call it when you flatly refused to discuss taking me on as a partner in Land's End?"

"I'd call it saving my ass and my sanity." Mike swung open the car door.

Jackie grabbed the steering wheel to prevent being deposited on her head in the snow. At the same time, she asserted herself.

"You can't do this to me."

"Watch me."

A second later his strong arms encircled her body and lifted her from the car. Seven voices rose in a cheering chorus. She threw a scorching look over Mike's shoulder at the men. They didn't even have the good grace to look admonished.

"Put me down!"

"All in good time."

"Put me down, now!"

"Gladly." None too gently, he dropped her onto

the driver's seat of the truck. "Shove your cute butt over. We're gonna have that talk you seem so all fired up about."

She threw him a hot glare and dug her feet in. "I'm not going anywhere but back inside my car. And if you think your caveman tactics will change my mind, you've got a lot to learn about me, buster."

His dark brows drew together in a threatening frown. Something told her that if she didn't do as he said, she would be in for a lot more trouble than she could handle. She shifted to the far side of the seat, just in time to make room for him to cram his body behind the steering wheel and close the door.

"Whose truck?" She didn't give a rat's patootie about the truck, but she needed time to marshal her thoughts.

"Mine. I keep it in the barn out back of the lodge. I only use it to go to town." His answer was clipped and to the point. "I should take you over my knee and give you what-for for trying to walk out on me."

"I already told you that your caveman tactics are not going to work."

He leaned close to her, nose to nose. "Since my caveman tactics won't work, let's try this."

Framing her face in his hands, he drew her lips to his and deposited a hard kiss on her mouth. She wiggled her toes inside her Gucci shoes. When he let her go, she flopped back against the seat, fighting for her equilibrium. Damn him!

"Good. Now that you're going to be quiet and listen—"

She sprang to attention. "Who said I was going to be quiet or that I'm interested in anything you have to say, you stubborn, opinionated—"

In a flash, Mike covered the space between them, then hauled her back into his arms for another stifling kiss. He leaned back and looked down at her. She opened her mouth to speak. "I have no objections to doing this for as long as it takes to convince you to hear me out."

As futile as she believed anything between them to be, God help her, she didn't object, either.

"Hell, we can keep doing it, anyway." His mouth covered hers again.

This time, his kiss swamped her with its sweet, slow intensity. Jackie's body turned to hot mush. Why fight something she wanted so desperately? Mike's arms around her. Mike's lips on hers.

He sprang back suddenly, as if he'd been burned. "Damn it, Jackie. Stop distracting me." He propelled himself backward to his side of the seat. "If I keep this up, I'll never say what I have to."

Shaking loose from the emotional cobwebs his kiss had woven around her, Jackie stole a glance at him. Lord, but she loved him, and because of that love, she'd come very close just now to surrendering to him and going along with whatever he wanted as long as they could be together.

But she couldn't. With each passing day, as Mike's resentfulness with his lot in life increased, the glitter of this moment would soon tarnish. His bitterness would turn him into an angry, unhappy man.

She needed better than that, deserved better. So did Mike, but if she couldn't save him from his misdirected loyalties, she could save herself from watching them eat him alive. Her capitulation right now would do nothing more than keep them both in an intolerable situation. But if his stubbornness kept him from admitting to or seeing it, then she would not be a party to it. He could talk to himself. She wanted out of this truck and out of his life, now, while she still had some of the pieces of her heart to hang on to.

"What if I don't want to listen? What if I just climb out of the truck and go back to my car?"

He turned a dead stare on her. "Try it."

She grabbed the door handle, but hesitated.

"Open it and before you can take two steps, I'll have your cute little backside on this seat again so fast you'll have to run to catch up with it."

The click of the door latch releasing echoed through the truck cab.

"Damn it, woman. I didn't spend the last three hours on the phone and half the morning sitting in a bank president's office so you could take off before I have my say." He reached across her lap and yanked the door closed, then slammed his hand down on the lock. "Now, sit back and listen."

She did as he demanded, surprised that a giggle had formed in her throat and was coming dangerously close to escaping.

"Here."

Tearing her gaze from the windshield, she looked

at his hand. It contained a large brown envelope. "What is it?"

"For once in your life, stop asking questions and just take it." He thrust it at her.

Slipping her fingers beneath the flap, she drew out the papers within. Her eyes grew wide. She opened her mouth to speak, but nothing came out. Dumbly, she turned to Mike.

"It's the deed to Land's End. We'll go to the bank tomorrow and sign the final papers." Mike glanced at her.

"But why?"

He slid his hand over his face, leaned his side against his door, then centered his gaze somewhere beyond the windshield. "When you talked about the plans you had for this place last night, I could hear the passion in your voice. I'll never feel like that about Land's End. Never could. Ken hadn't even sounded like that. I'm signing it over to you. It's yours."

How had he known? Until this very second, Jackie had no idea how much converting Land's End to the inner-city family camp had meant to her. But Mike knew. And where would he go, now that he'd made up his mind to cut loose from Ken's dream?

"There's one catch."

"Oh?" Jackie held her breath.

"I go with the deal."

Joy shot through her like a lightning bolt. Happiness bubbled over. "I wouldn't have it any other way." She launched herself across the seat into

Mike's waiting arms, then covered his face with kisses. "We'll make wonderful partners. You'll see."

"No. Not partners."

The joy subsided. What did he mean? She pulled back, not knowing what to expect, but mentally preparing herself for another mortal blow. "I don't understand."

"First of all, as much as I want you in my arms, you have to promise to stay on your side of the seat for a little while. Just until I tell you what I have to."

He watched her obediently wiggle across the seat. With any luck, he could get through this without throwing her over his shoulder like some Neanderthal and finding a cave to make love to her until neither of them had the strength to stand.

"The phone call I made was to the president of the bank just before I went to his office and arranged for the transfer of the property to you. But it was also to find out if the loan had to be used for improvements to Land's End. He assured me I could use it for what I have in mind."

"That's good, because I wouldn't have wanted you to..." The scowl he aimed at her effectively silenced her.

"The second phone call I made was to Albany, to the Department of Forestry, to get information for enrolling in college to work with the Forestry Service."

Her face reflected absolute joy at his announcement. She made a move to throw herself back in his arms. As much as he wanted her there, needed her there, he put up a hand to ward her off. He had to say it all now, while he could.

"You can have Land's End to do whatever you want with. I'll always be nearby for help and support, but I have to do this other thing for myself.

"The long and short of it is, that if I went along with your plan, I'd be trading Ken's dream for yours. I knew that almost as soon as I really thought about what you were proposing. I need my own dream. If you haven't hammered anything else into my thick skull in the past weeks, you've gotten that much through to me."

Jackie laid her hand on his, where it rested on the gearshift. "What about Ken?"

"Ken is dead. It's time I faced that. Maybe if I'd made it to the hospital in time to say goodbye, maybe I'd have been able to change the way things turned out. Then again, maybe not. Maybe I'd have done it all the same. We'll never know, and there's no use worrying about it." He ran his free hand through his hair. "All I know is that without you here to share whatever I choose to do, it doesn't mean a whole lot."

Unable to put it off another minute, he dragged her into his arms and kissed her thoroughly. He framed her face in his big hands and traced her fine cheekbones with his thumbs.

"I love you, Jackie. I want you here, as my wife, raising our kids, helping me to teach them to love the mountains and everything in them, showering them with your special kind of love. But most of all, I want to grow old looking into your beautiful face and holding your warmth next to me through the night after a day that becomes too much to bear. I want to make snow angels with you and share our dreams—yours, mine and ours."

Tears welled in her eyes, then trickled down her cheeks. He wiped at them with his thumbs. Her face broke into a smile that etched itself across his heart.

"Oh, Mike, that's all I ever wanted for us. I love you so much and I can't think of a better way to grow old than in your arms."

He leaned forward to kiss her, then remembered one other thing. "About your money. I can't do much about you having it, but I won't have you using it to finance any part of my schooling. I'll use the loan the bank gave me. I know you're used to fine things and living high, but that's not me and it's not part of the life up here in the mountains. What you've seen in the past few weeks is pretty much as exciting as it gets."

She stopped his words with a gentle kiss. "First of all, from my perspective, things were *plenty* exciting." She wiggled her eyebrows at him. "Secondly, I'm no more used to high living than you are."

What in hell was she getting at? A blind man could see she had boatloads of bucks. "I don't understand."

"About three months ago I won the New York State lottery. I'm...uh, I believe the term is 'filthy rich.'"

Mike felt his jaw drop. "You're that rich?"

She stared at him as if he'd grown an extra head.

"This should hardly come as a surprise to you, of all people. Wasn't it you who made all those charming comments about my luggage and car?"

"Yes. But that was all before I knew you were *that* rich ."

She frowned and leaned away from him. "Yes. I'm that rich."

"Filthy rich," he said again, feeling as if he'd just been the recipient of a stomach punch. "And you didn't come up here to escape the lifestyles of the rich and famous?"

Slowly, almost cautiously, she shook her head. "No. The only thing I was trying to escape was the hoopla of the media. I hated being rich, but what I hated even more was having my private life invaded and splashed all over the newspapers."

Mike felt the laughter bubble up in him like a spring. It burst forth and filled the truck's cab. Jackie eyed him quizzically. Obviously, he wasn't reacting as she'd expected him to. "This is unbelievable," he sputtered between more fits of laughter. "Does anyone else know?"

"No. I let you and everyone but Harold believe that I was born to the Fortune 500."

"Why not Harold?"

"I hired Harold as my accountant. I guess you could say we sort of traded talents."

"Aha! The dinner?" When she nodded, he grinned. "Well, that sure explains a lot. Your clothes, the car, the luggage. Somehow I never felt it fitted you." He chuckled.

"Would you mind telling me why you find this whole thing so damn funny?"

He threw his arm around her and gathered her against his chest. "Ever since I first saw you, I've been lecturing myself about how ill suited we were. About how far out of my league you were. Now, when I've finally convinced myself that I can overlook your money and pray that you can settle into a less than extravagant lifestyle, you tell me you've only been rich for three months." He sighed, thinking about all the wasted time. "But if you were so unhappy about being rich, why did you buy all that flashy hardware? The car. The luggage. The clothes."

She laughed. "My helpful brother bought them for me. You see, he's the one who let it drop about who I was to the media and turned my life into a beehive. The fancy trappings are Dave's warped idea of an apology. I'm a sweatshirt-and-jeans gal."

She looped her arms around his neck and snuggled into his side. "I'm afraid you'll just be marrying a cook. One that's rich as hell, but, nevertheless, a cook."

"That's fine with me," he said, kissing her heartily.

Things were quickly falling into place. All those unexplainable aspects of Jackie that he'd questioned—her laid-back attitude, her willingness to sit on the ice and bait her own hook, her uncanny waitressing abilities. All the things that didn't jibe with the Jackie he'd come to know and love.

Recent wealth he could handle. It was the old,

snooty rich that felt the world owed them veneration that made the hairs on his neck stand at attention. However, he was curious as to how much "filthy rich" consisted of. "Just how much money are we talking about here?"

"More than you can possibly imagine. Enough to rebuild Land's End, to keep it open and running and finance whole families to come here for a week, year-round. And that won't even put a healthy dent in it." She looked into his eyes for a few moments. "Mike, is my money going to be a problem for us? Because if it is, I'll give it all away."

He kissed her for her generous nature. "No need to do that. I can't foresee any problems. The money itself was never really my hang-up. I've come to understand that. It's the things it does to people that's the problem." He leaned back and looked into her face. "But I can't see anything changing you. Unless it's too much work with this plan of yours. Do you have any idea of the size of the project you're taking on?"

"No. And telling me won't scare me off. I consider the contract we've made to be lifelong, irreversible and very, very binding."

She wrinkled her nose and kissed him again. He liked her brand of persuasion.

"Thank God." Then, with all the pent-up longing that he'd kept tamped for too long given free rein, he kissed her. Neither money, nor Land's End entered his mind. It was too full of Jackie and their love.

Epilogue

For the second time in her life, Jackie Hamilton awoke to find herself surrounded by men. Unlike the first time, smiles wreathed their clean-shaven faces, and Peppy's grin was the widest of all.

Since their collective heads blocked the sunlight streaming through her window, she couldn't see their faces all that clearly, but she knew each and every one of them as well as she knew herself. So dear. So much a part of her life. She still missed their beards, but they'd been adamant about not scaring the babies with their furry faces and had begun shaving regularly right after she'd announced she was expecting. But they'd promised to grow them back in a few months.

One other change from the first time stood out. This time, there were eight faces, instead of seven—the eighth belonging to her darling husband, Mike. Since they'd converted Land's End into the year-round retreat for inner-city families and he'd entered Forestry School, he'd become a relaxed, happy, contented man who shared his love of nature and his beloved mountains with everyone. When he wasn't working at the local office for the Forestry Service, attending classes, or assigned to one of his month-long vigils in the fire tower, he was helping Adam, who lived at the camp year-round—as did Doc, Harold, and Tony—plan his nature hikes for their guests.

"How are you feeling?" Doc took her wrist between his thumb and forefinger and felt for her pulse.

"Fine. Tired, but fine."

"I'm not surprised. It's not every woman who can give birth to twins and get up to dance the jig." He stepped back, adjusted his glasses, then glanced at the others. "Now, don't tire her out more with a lot of silly chatter. She needs her rest."

One by one, they filed past her bed, depositing a kiss on her cheek and a bouquet of flowers in her arms. By the time they'd all paid homage to the new mother, she looked like an entry in the Rose Bowl Parade, and smelled like it, too.

Mike leaned down and kissed her softly. "Kim says the boys are bathed and ready to meet their godfathers."

She smiled. The boys. Her sons. Their sons. Hers and Mike's. Just thinking the words filled her with warm fuzzies.

Kim and Tommy came in carrying two small blue bundles. Stark terror claimed Tommy's features. He clutched the baby close to his chest and walked as cautiously as if he carried a cup of steaming coffee and didn't want to spill any. Carefully, he lowered his burden into Jackie's waiting arms, then stepped back and heaved a sigh of relief.

Kim transferred her baby to Mike. She turned and grinned down at Jackie. "Thank goodness they aren't identical. At least you'll be spared all those horrid tricks twins play on their parents."

Jackie chuckled and looked down at her pink-faced son. "I'm sure they'll find other ways to torture us." The baby cooed and wiggled. Jackie brushed aside the leaf of a yellow carnation that tickled the baby's cheek.

"Get those flowers off the bed. Can't have them contaminating my godson," Peppy grumbled, scooping up an armful of the bouquets and piling them on a chair atop an unsuspecting, snoozing Rip.

"Your godson?" Adam stepped forward, hands on hips. "What about my godson?" His cheeks grew red, almost as red as his abused nose.

When she'd had the sonogram done and found she would be having twin boys, Jackie had been afraid of this happening. She'd agreed to name the boys after their seven friends if they didn't fight about it. Needless to say, there had been innumerable squabbles about the babies ever since. Although none of them had been designated godfather to any particular child, they seem to have gravitated toward the child that carried their name.

She looked down at her sleeping son. No child would ever be loved more than Kenneth Michael Jacob Adam Thomas Hamilton and David William Anthony Preston Harold Hamilton. Since everyone but Peppy, Rip and Tommy lived at Land's End year-round, the babies would have godfathers galore to spoil them, love them and teach them their wisdom.

Despite what it had done to Mike's nervous system and the clamoring of the seven men it had produced, she was glad the unexpected March storm had blocked the road last night and the boys had had to be delivered at home. Having Doc bring her sons into the world made them much more special to her and Mike, and drew her little family of friends and loved ones closer still.

Tommy stepped forward, carrying two small bouquets of violets. Shyly, he gave them to Jackie, then stared down at the baby. "He's so small."

"They tend to come that way." Harold rubbed at his protruding middle. "It's only after they get growing that they put on the pounds." Grinning at Jackie, he raised an eyebrow at the boy. "Of course, eating Jackie's cooking doesn't hurt, either."

Jackie and Mike exchanged grins, but she made a mental note to speak to Doc about a fat-free menu. Most of the men had put on weight since living at Land's End on a permanent basis, which spoke well for her cooking, but not for their health.

Otherwise, life was wonderful. Each man made his contribution to the running of the camp. Tony counseled the families and children, sending them home refreshed mentally, as well as physically. Adam, when not conducting nature walks, taught fishing and fly-tying. Doc, with Kim working as his resident nursing assistant, took care of everyone's physical well-being. And Harold reveled in the avalanche of accounting chores, as well as the food. Rip participated long distance by keeping the camp in the public eye through his advertising agency.

Peppy had moved to a nearby town right after his youngest daughter left for college. Jackie, after seeing the beautiful layette Martha had stitched to go with the handmade cradles the seven godfathers had crafted, was thinking of asking her to teach sewing.

Tommy couldn't seem to stay away from Kim for very long, so he divided his vacations between home and the camp and helped Doc in the infirmary.

Land's End was everything and more than she'd envisioned. She looked at Mike, who was staring in wonder at his son. Thanks to this man, she had a life richer than any lottery could ever make it.

"I'm so glad you were here when the boys came." She smiled up at her handsome husband. "Who's on duty at the tower?"

"Chuck. When I called and said you'd gone into labor early, they sent up a replacement for me. I'm off till the end of the month." He grinned and winked. "Of course, I'm going to miss your impromptu visits."

"Hey, don't knock my visits, Mr. Hamilton. If you count back nine months, you'll find one of them paid off in a very special way."

Mike leaned over, placed the baby in the crook of her free arm, then deposited a kiss on her upturned lips. "Indeed it did, Mrs. Hamilton. Indeed it did."

He sat carefully on the edge of the bed and surveyed his riches. Jackie might be the one with all the bucks in the family, but he wouldn't trade one of his treasures for all of hers. "Have I told you lately how much I love you?"

"Yes, but you can say it again. I never tire of hearing you say it."

"Ahem!"

They looked toward the men gathered at the foot of the bed.

"I think we'll be going now. Lots of work to be done before the next group of families arrive, right, boys?" Doc fingered his glasses back to the bridge of his nose, then began herding the others from the room. They all smiled and waved to Jackie. "See you later."

Jackie and Mike laughed aloud. The babies flinched at the sound. Mike inhaled the mixture of Jackie's perfume and baby talc. What an exotic combination. "Do you think they'll ever get tired of playing matchmakers?"

"I doubt it." She shifted the baby to a more comfortable position. "If you ask them how we ended up married, each of them has their own version of why he, and he alone, is responsible for us ending up together."

Slipping the other baby from his mother's arms and laying both in the waiting cradles, Mike returned to the side of the bed. He reclined against the pillows and gathered his wife tenderly to him. "Little do they know that we ended up together because we couldn't stay apart," he whispered huskily, then deposited a kiss to the top of her head.

She shifted to her side and snuggled her face into his shoulder. The love emanating from her filled and warmed him. Not long ago he didn't have a dream to call his own. Now, thanks to his beloved Jackie, he had more dreams than he could count.

"I love you, Mike Hamilton, even if sometimes you're a—"

He silenced her with his mouth…just as she knew he would.

On the plus side, you've raised a
wonderful, strong-willed daughter.
On the minus side, she's using that
determination to find

A Match For MOM

Three very different stories of mothers,
daughters and heroes...from three of your
all-time favorite authors:

GUILTY
by Anne Mather

A MAN FOR MOM
by Linda Randall Wisdom

THE FIX-IT MAN
by Vicki Lewis Thompson

Available this May wherever
Harlequin and Silhouette books are sold.

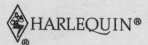 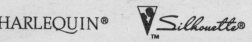

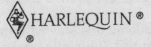

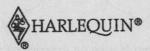